ICE CAVE

TOBY J. NICHOLS

SEVERED PRESS
HOBART TASMANIA

ICE CAVE

Copyright © 2020 Toby J. Nichols
Copyright © 2020 by Severed Press

WWW.SEVEREDPRESS.COM

ISBN: 978-1-922323-27-9

CHAPTER 1

The view from the camp on Mount Erebus was stunning. There was no other way to describe it. The world was sharp white and crisp blue. The air was cold enough to cut Saxon Smith's lungs with each breath. After two days acclimatizing to the thinner air, he was ready for a new challenge—the descent into the ice caves. But he wanted to take in every moment of the view because once inside, the only thing he'd be seeing was rock and ice.

He was hoping to find life.

This expedition could be what took his life from unrecognized lab assistant to feted researcher—like Brian Meyer. He'd been to Antarctica so many times he didn't care about the view. He chatted about previous expeditions as if they were nothing. He didn't seem to care that he was ever here. But to Saxon, this would never get old.

He drew in a breath and closed his eyes, giving himself a moment to live his dream now that he was on the cusp of making it happen. His parents hadn't wanted him to go to uni; they called his job a waste of time. This trip, he'd show them that what he did was valuable.

He'd discover a new species, write papers, and research. Be an expert and in demand to give lectures. He'd be able to come back again and again. The shine faded off his dream and he opened his eyes. Coming on this trip had caused a fight with Doug that he hadn't expected.

"Yeah, I was once caught in a blizzard. We couldn't do anything for days. Got to know each other really well." Brian nodded to Vivian.

Even through the tinted goggles, Saxon could see her roll her eyes. Viv Anstruther seemed ready to shove Brian down the mountain and not look back. Saxon shook his head. If Brian started on about his divorce again—to make it totally clear he was single—Carmel had said they would all agree Brian fell repeatedly on his ice pick.

Carmel Emerson had celebrated her thirty-fifth birthday the day before they were choppered up the side of Erebus and had been spared Brian's attention. Whether it was because of her age, her glare, or simple luck, Saxon had no idea. While he was a biologist, he'd never studied women and wasn't about to start.

The next week would be spent exploring as much as they could and taking samples from deep in the cave system. One of the reasons Saxon had been asked was because he climbed in his spare time. The other was because of Carmel who had been his mentor on his first field trip to the southern end of Tasmania. He was the one with the least experience and they all knew it.

"Let's got a move on." Saxon grinned behind his balaclava. They were exploring unknown parts of the world. His family sneered at his degree, laughed at the trip. They wouldn't laugh when he came back loaded with scientific accolades. Well, they probably would, but others wouldn't. He was going to be someone.

Brian glared at him. "You aren't the leader. I am."

Saxon lowered his gaze. An apology formed on his lips, but he didn't say it. He wanted Brian to view him as a colleague, not the green kid that was being dragged along because he knew how to use a rope. "I'm just keen to see what's in there."

The first expedition had found DNA that wasn't on any database. Maybe they'd find what it belonged to since they were going deeper than any other team—their mission was to find the warm ecosystems deep beneath the ice.

When Brian declared that they were ready, they set off into Mount Erebus. They spent most of the first day winding through tunnels that glowed eerie blue as the light filtered through the ice. When they stopped, they took samples of soil and rock, but if anything was alive, it must be microscopic. Saxon was hoping for something more exciting than a microbe—though plenty of people loved them. They needed to go deeper where it was warmer and get into the caverns.

Antarctica was riddled with volcanos. For all anyone knew, the entire continent was sitting on a honeycomb of ice caves—each one an enclosed ecosystem that could harbor unique organisms that had once evolved from some common ancestor that had been long forgotten. That's what made him excited and why he'd said yes when it would've been easier to say no.

Carmel mapped as they went, making notes every time they picked one tunnel over another—usually because Brian said so. Winding deeper into the mountain, eventually, they found a tunnel that led down.

This time, he spoke up. "I want to take a look."

A previous expedition had guessed it was as warm as twenty degrees Celsius in some places. That was practically tropical down here.

"I know you want to find something more than single-cell organisms, but if we go down, how do we get back up?" Brian asked. He wanted to stick to the upper tunnels, even though they weren't warm enough, and this trip was to find warm environments. Saxon couldn't figure out why. "We should continue on."

"Saxon's right," Carmel said.

He smiled even though she couldn't see it and faced Brian. "It's a gentle slope."

Until it wouldn't be. But he'd put in ice screws and a rope for guidance, and they could put on crampons and they all carried picks. "We can leave our supplies here if you don't want to carry everything." If they left their camping gear, they'd be able to move faster. He only wanted to take a look. If it seemed promising, they could come back and camp here for the night then continue. They'd hit a few dead ends today, and this would probably be no different.

"We'll be back in an hour," Viv added.

Three of them wanted to explore. If Brian vetoed Viv, he'd never get in her sleeping bag.

Brian put his hands on his hips as though considering their options. "I was hoping to go in more before we went down, but we can look. We'll waste what's left of the day, but no longer." He shrugged off his pack and pulled the much smaller day pack out, which he filled with food and water.

The rest of them did the same.

Saxon couldn't understand why Brian wasn't jumping at the chance to do something new. It seemed like all he cared about was hitting on Viv and talking about his past glories. Is that what happened when you became so well known? You stopped caring about the science? He wouldn't become like that. But he wanted to find enough so he could come back again. He was already thinking of more trips.

Saxon added extra food and rope and made sure he had a small first-aid kit. He'd done enough climbs to err on the side of redundancy. Everyone had a rope and harness and while getting kitted up would be a pain, if the tunnel became steep and icy, they'd all be thankful.

Brian put his backpack on. "Aren't you going to put a screw in?"

Saxon hesitated. He had a limited number, and he didn't want to waste them. "Not yet, it's a gentle walk."

Brian grunted. "Lead on, since you want to do this."

That wasn't exactly approval, but it was near enough.

The ice was mesmerizing, but he didn't dawdle. Couldn't. Not if he wanted to get as far as possible in his limited time.

Carmel caught up with him. "He's pissed with you."

"I didn't come here to walk around and pretend to do science. We should be doing more than mapping tunnels." The frustration that had been simmering boiled over.

"None of us did, but Brian *knows* people."

Saxon glanced at her. Brian had made it clear that he was something big, and that he could make or break their careers. He needed the hand up, and this was it. If Carmel couldn't afford to piss off Brian, he definitely couldn't. "Do you think I pushed too hard?"

"No…but let me make the next suggestion. Viv wants more than a frosty vacation too. I think we're all on the same page so if we back each other up, it will be okay."

Until they got home, and Brian made a few phone calls and life got hard. Saxon needed to make more connections, but it wasn't easy.

Laughter rolled down the tunnel.

Carmel glanced back. "She wasn't quick enough this time."

"She should definitely report him." Saxon didn't want to get caught up in the Viv-Brian mess either. He changed the topic. "There's no rock here."

The smooth icy sides of the tunnel left nothing for life to cling to.

"Not yet...how deep do you think this goes?" Carmel asked as though quizzing him on something he should know, the way she once had.

"Maybe we're right in the heart of a massive ice sheet." He grinned. "Is it warmer?"

"I don't know." She checked her equipment. "Yeah. It's a massive five degrees. Probably because we're deep in the mountain. I don't think it's to do with the heat source."

The heat source being the active volcano whose steam had scoured out the ice to create the tunnels they'd been exploring all day.

If it erupted, they'd be toast.

"Look, dirt!" Carmel walked faster and made her way over to the small patch of black soil. She collected a sample, taking photos and notes and marking the location.

Something caught the corner of his gaze and he turned. "What was that?"

Carmel looked up. "What?"

There was nothing there. Maybe the weird blue light was playing tricks on his eyes. But he walked around the corner where the shadow had vanished, going deeper on his own. There was nothing there. He was seeing things. Farther on, the tunnel ahead got steeper and narrower. There were rocks overhead and to the left. While Carmel did the science, he put a screw into the righthand side and knotted a rope to form the start of a handrail.

Viv and Brian were chatting like old friends—she did a good job of putting up with him and keeping him on her side. He needed to make more of an effort, so that when they got home, the calls Brian made about him were recommendations.

Saxon turned. "Did you want to lead, Brian?"

Saxon froze. He had seen something. It was almost invisible against the dark rock. He'd walked right under what had to be a thirty-centimeter centipede that shouldn't even be living here. He shuddered, glad that he was wearing multiple layers of clothing.

"No, you're the mountain goat." Brian laughed at his own joke.

"What is it?" Viv walked toward Saxon.

He pointed up, but she wouldn't be able to see from where she was standing. The rock was in the way. "Come around the right, slowly."

Brian muttered about the hold up.

Viv edged around until she stood next to Saxon. "That's a big one."

"Yeah. I didn't bring anything to hold something that size." None of them had. He took a photo. His hand unsteady...had he just made his first discovery? "You want to hold up the scale."

"You saw it, you do it."

Hopefully, the centipede wouldn't land on him—he didn't want to find out how poisonous its bite was. Three more photos and it was still clinging to the rocks like it was waiting for the humans to piss off. "I should collect it."

Brian stomped over. "What is it?" His mouth hung open as he saw the insect. He huffed. "Well...I'm sure there's plenty of them around."

"This isn't a nematode." Nematodes lived in Antarctica; centipedes didn't. Or no one knew they had until today. Saxon wasn't a fan of invertebrates, but if that's what made him famous, he'd take it and love it and research it and write papers on it. "It's a centipede...they don't live here." Except clearly, they did where it was warmer. "I guess there'll be more of them as we head down."

"You want to go deeper? Do we need to?" Brian kept his gaze on the centipede.

"Brian, you can't walk away from this chance. Saxon found a centipede—there could be all kinds of things down there." Viv kept her voice sweet, but there was something else in it that Saxon couldn't work out.

Carmel joined them and slapped Saxon on the shoulder. "Well spotted. We should have brought tubs for critters."

"Yeah." Saxon smiled and glanced up at his centipede.

"If we find more, you should kill one and bring it back anyway."

He nodded, not sure he wanted to put that in his bag—he could always empty the first-aid kid and use that box in a pinch.

They made their way deeper into the mountain, always heading down. Gradually, the slope became more extreme. They were scientists, not cavers...Saxon knew enough to get by, but he was no expert. Was Brian right about staying nearer the top?

Saxon put another screw into the ice wall and threaded the rope though. They were all using it as a handrail, but one wrong step and it would be a slide to God knows where. "I think we should clip on."

"That means putting the harnesses on?" Viv asked.

"Yeah." He looked at the three other scientists. If they said no, he wouldn't push. It would be a mistake to make them go out of their comfort zone.

"I'm not putting on a harness. We should turn back," Brian said. "Check out other branches of the tunnel system."

"A bit further...we haven't seen anything else," Carmel said. "Maybe the centipedes live up there and there are other things down here. It wouldn't be a monoculture of just centipedes."

If there was a centipede, there had to be things for it to eat...and things that would eat it. He glanced at the rock wall and ceiling. Maybe they lived in the rock, squeezing through hidden gaps. Its body was as thick as his thumb, but flattish. Not like the ones he remembered seeing growing up.

He wanted to know what else was down here, but he didn't say that. So far, it was one against and one for. Viv had the deciding vote. "What about you, Viv?"

"The next team will go further than us...you don't want them finding something cool just because we didn't go an extra few meters." She pulled her balaclava down and tossed Brian a smile. "Or you could wait here while we go on?"

Brian's resistance melted like ice in the summer sun. Yeah, he wanted to get into her pants, but she knew how to use that to get Brian on an invisible leash. They spend the next few minutes getting geared up. Brian kept glancing around like he expected something to drop out of the ceiling.

"I don't think he likes caves," Saxon muttered to Carmel.

"Then he should've let someone else come on this expedition." She shrugged. "With his name, he can do whatever he wants anyway."

"Then why did you agree?"

"Because I wanted the opportunity."

He'd accepted the job for the same reason.

They made their way down the slope, Saxon at the lead. Sweat formed beneath the layers of clothing. It had been five degrees, but he was sure it was more than that now.

They rounded a corner where the blue glow of sunlight filtered through the ice dimmed. The walls were mostly rock. Where there was rock, there might be dirt and microbes. They shed their packs and took samples, inspected every crevice with a torch.

Saxon unzipped his jacket and took off his gloves. The air was cool, but not bitter and frozen. If there was going to be life—life other than centipedes—they must be on top of it.

Brian sat down and ate and drank. Saxon went a little bit ahead to find a location for the next screw. Ahead, the tunnel lightened again, still heading down like they were heading toward the center of the earth.

A small noise, like nails being dropped, drew his attention. He peered closer at the wall. A knot of the centipedes writhed over something smaller. For several seconds, he stared, unable to move. There really was life in the caves.

"There are more centipedes," he called out. Was it a new species or a remnant from back when Antarctica was joined to Australia and Patagonia? Either way, no one had expected something this big to be alive in the tunnels. Antarctica was a desert and most life, like the seals and birds and whales, clung to the watery edges. The warmth down here could harbor anything.

A small laugh escaped, and he didn't know if it was from nerves or excitement. They had found something, the start of something big he was sure. He blinked and imagined the accolades. His parents would be stunned, of course. They stop telling him to get a real job where he got his hands dirty. Doug would apologize and realize that Saxon's work was important. He'd publish articles and get invited to speak overseas—Doug would just have to accept that he wasn't the only one who traveled for work.

The hairs along his arm prickled, and he opened his eyes. The centipedes were still eating. He looked up, wondering how deep they were beneath the rock and ice. His heart hammered and the old fear of being trapped flooded him. He drew in a breath and smothered it—calling for help, begging to be let out had never earned him anything but more punishment. He didn't like confined spaces that much, but already this trip had been worth it. Besides, it wasn't a confined space. There was plenty of air and room to move. He drew in another breath, then watched one centipede wriggle away. There was enough of them for him to get a sample. It would fit in the first-aid kit and be better to study than a photo.

Brian checked his watch. He was pale and sweaty. "Half an hour, we still have to walk back."

"I know," Saxon said as he carefully put the dead centipede away. What were the centipedes been eating? Each other? "But I think we're getting close."

There was something else down here. There had to be.

He skirted the still feeding centipedes. The next part of the tunnel was crystalline blue, like something out of a fairytale. The walls and ceiling glittered, and Saxon paused to absorb the fact that he was the first person to ever step foot in here. He was an explorer, a scientist. And no one could take that away from him, though he could already hear his father's mocking voice. The sneers that he had soft hands from living in a lab. He hadn't taken this trip to prove himself...he'd come to make discoveries. And he'd done that already. He didn't need to go deeper or find more things, but at the same time, he didn't want to leave and go down what could be dead ends...or there could be even better discoveries down other tunnels. He drew in a breath, his body vibrating with possibilities. He'd forgotten what it was like to do fieldwork.

The ice groaned like a giant waking from slumber. If the volcano beneath their feet erupted, they were dead, but at least it would be quick. He kneeled to have a drink and a bite of food, carefully putting his rubbish in his bag. In his heavy winter clothing, he was sweating, which wouldn't be good when he got back outside. He peeled off the top and tied the arms around his waist, then changed his mind and took the whole outer layer off.

Fuck it. He was here. He'd make the most of it.

"I'm going to clip in and do a quick run deeper." He pulled on his harness and triple-checked everything, before putting his small backpack on and sliding the loop of his ice pick around his wrist.

Brian glared at him. "Why?"

"Because we're here. No one else has to come. I'm being safe."

"Trying to be a hero," Brian muttered.

Saxon shook his head; he didn't want to put Brian offside. "Half an hour you said, that's all I'll be."

"I'll come with," Viv called. "Just make sure my clothes don't get full of centipedes."

Brian shot her a glare that she ignored as Saxon checked her harness, then they made their way deeper. Every so often, Saxon would add another ice screw. He didn't know what he was hoping to find, only that if he had half an hour to explore, it was better to use it than sit around their makeshift camp listening to Brian talk about his previous exploits.

"What do you think is down here?" Viv asked as they put some distance between Brian and Carmel.

"I don't know. Something. It's warm, so there'll be melted ice to make water. Could be anything. Something no one has ever seen." Or nothing. This could be a risky waste of time and effort.

"No sun."

"But there is light. Enough for mosses and lichen to grow?" He shrugged, then his foot slipped on the ice. He skidded on his ass before jamming the pick into the ice and halting his slide. His heart pounded on his ribs and for a few seconds, he forgot how to breathe. The tunnel went on forever, disappearing into darkness.

"Shit, are you okay?"

"Fine." His heart was beating faster than a frightened rabbit's, but he was physically fine. He couldn't have gone far. "Nothing broken."

Viv carefully walked over then put out her hand. He took it and stood.

The ice creaked beneath his feet. He glanced down and saw cracks spreading where he'd jammed the pick into the floor of the tunnel. He released her hand. "Get back!"

"What?" Then she looked down. Her eyes widened, and she edged back toward the wall and the rope that led back to Brian and Carmel.

He couldn't follow her because the cracks were widening between them, so he edged back to the other wall. The rope connecting him to safety stretched out. He hoped he'd done everything right. He was sure he had. He remembered the way Doug had shown him what to do the first day they'd met. They hadn't made up.

A chunk of ice fell out of the floor and vanished. He never heard it stop falling. And his heart fell with it. He'd broken the cave, and everything was falling to the center of the earth. Another chunk fell away.

"Go. Follow the rope back," he said.

"I'm not leaving you."

"I'll be right behind you." He gripped his rope as more of the floor fell away.

She took a few steps away then stopped and glanced back. "I can hear screaming."

Over the cracking of the ice, so could he.

CHAPTER 2

Saxon glanced at the ever-widening hole, then back up the tunnel where the screaming was coming from. What had happened to Brian and Carmel?

"We shouldn't have left them," Viv said, but she didn't move any closer toward them.

"There was nothing up there…except the centipedes."

Carmel ran down the corridor, no longer attached. Her feet slipped, but she didn't slow. "They're attacking us."

"Stop," Saxon shouted, his voice ringing off the ice.

Viv lunged toward Carmel and grabbed her before she could run straight into the hole. But their combined weight made Viv slide closer to the fragile edge.

"They dropped out of nowhere, dozens of them," Carmel panted. "I think I got bitten."

Viv tried to calm Carmel. "There's nothing on you. You're fine."

"Centipedes don't bite, they stab with their front legs..." Saxon frowned. "Where's Brian?" He had a vision of him buried under a knot of writhing centipedes. It was enough to make his stomach turn and his skin twitch.

"Get them off me." Brian thundered down the tunnel, not caring about safety or anything else.

Saxon stepped out to stop Brian from falling into the hole. "Stop. Look down."

But it was too late.

Brian barreled into Saxon and they both went through the hole. The rope unraveled fast, and there was nothing Saxon could do but grab onto Brian so he didn't fall. The rope jerked. Saxon's teeth clacked together and then the two men swung. For several heartbeats, he enjoyed the fact he was still alive. He drew in a slow breath and tried to think what to do next. He didn't have long before he lost his grip on Brian. In front of him was a rock wall, but it was too far to reach. Then he became aware that something was crawling along his arm and he could feel every leg through his thin thermal undershirt. He wished he had his thick snow suit on.

Brian slipped, and he whimpered. "Do something."

"Just hold on." Saxon tried to glance down to gauge the drop, hoping they could just land, but they were swaying, and Brian was in the way. The centipede was on his upper arm now.

If the ice cut the rope, they were dangling on...

"Carmel, Viv. I need another rope."

The harness bit into the wrong parts of him. Brian scrabbled at his legs, trying to keep ahold. The centipede made its way over Saxon's neck, and the hairs all over his body stood on end. Were there more of them down here?

A nest of hard black bodies beneath them? He closed his eyes for a moment, then made sure to keep his gaze up. They both dropped as another chunk of ice on the edge of the hole fell away.

Saxon's heart beat hard and high in his throat.

Every time the hole widened, they swung closer to the cliff face.

"Where's the damn rope?"

"Coming. Just securing the end," Carmel called.

Saxon's grip on Brian was weakening. "We're going to get to the cliff face." That would buy them a few handholds and time. But it would also mean deliberately swinging and possibly widening the hole and wearing the rope on the ice.

Brian's nails dug into Saxon's thighs. "I'll fall."

"Then we'd better make it fast." The centipede dropped over his forehead and it was all Saxon could do to hold on to Brian and not bat the thing away. A rope descended about a meter away.

"There's a ledge not far below you," Viv called.

Saxon peered down and thought he saw green below, but he couldn't be sure. "Brian, how for below is the ledge?"

Brian clawed at Saxon's pants like he wanted to climb up him. "I can't look down. I don't like heights."

"The end of the rope is touching the ledge," Carmel added.

"Grab the rope and climb down." The rope they were on jerked again as more ice fell away. "Grab the fucking rope, or I'm letting go." He eased the grip of the hand that wasn't doing much to hold Brian anyway.

It was enough for Brian to find the will to reach out and grab the rope. "I'm going to fall and die."

"You won't die." He shut his mouth fast before the centipede got any closer and breathed carefully through his nose. Would it fit up his nose? He didn't want to find out. With his free hand, he reached up and yanked it off his face, tossing it as far away as he could. But he could still feel its legs on his skin, and he wanted to scratch all over. He hoped there'd been only one.

Where the hell were the others that had been on Brian? With luck, they'd dropped off when they'd fallen through the ice.

Brian slid down Saxon's leg, one hand on the rope, the other dragging down Saxon's pants.

"Two hands on the rope." He needed Brian off him before the harness cut off circulation to his junk.

"Then what?"

"Then you climb down…knees on the rope."

Brian gazed up at him. "Easy for you…you have a harness."

At that moment, he'd have rather just had a rope. "There's a ledge below you. It's not far. And Viv is watching." *Sorry, Viv.*

Brian looked up at the hole they'd fallen through. It wasn't that far, maybe a ten-meter climb. But there was no way Brian could make it without a harness and someone assisting. He tried to breathe calmly; this would be fine. They'd sort this out and head back to the rest of their gear and laugh about it as they ate their heat and eat meals.

If he hadn't insisted on going just a bit farther…

"I'll play out what's left of my rope and drop down to the ledge." Hopefully, he'd have enough. He didn't want to scrape Brian off him, but this was becoming more uncomfortable by the heartbeat.

Brian put both hands on the second rope. The relief for Saxon was immediate, but not enough. He wanted his feet on something solid and to do a quick centipede check. Brian was attempting to climb down, but it was more of an assisted fall. He landed heavily on the ledge, but the rock held. Saxon sighed with relief and made his way down.

"Are you two okay down there?" Carmel called.

Brian had his back pressed to the rock wall, eyes wide.

"Great," Saxon lied. He was dangling a foot over a ledge, because his rope wasn't quite long enough. He stretched his foot out and used it to spin so he could see what was behind him— hopefully, nothing that wanted to eat him.

If more ice broke off, he'd have enough rope to land safely—if he didn't smash into the wall hard. He turned to face the cavern.

Cavern was too small...cathedral might be better. It was huge, lit from the surface with soft, blue, ice-filtered light. The air had lost the bite and was warm, properly warm, and laden with the scent of vegetation. He lowered his gaze to take in the green swathe that covered the floor. He blinked and then blinked again. Trees. This wasn't a lichen carpet or even a fungus, but actual goddamn trees.

He glanced up. "Carmel...you're going to want to see this."

"What is it? Did you discover another centipede?"

"Trees. There're trees down here." And he hung there, forgetting about the way the harness bit into his thigh and balls as he stared at the lush, dark-green foliage. Everyone thought the Antarctic forests had died millennia ago, and he was staring at a remnant. A forgotten fragment.

A lost world.

He closed his eyes, then opened them to be sure he hadn't just imagined it. He was reasonably sure that he wasn't dead either. They'd found a forest trapped beneath a dome of ice. And no one back home would believe them if they didn't get photos and samples.

"You're going to want to get down here," he called to Viv and Carmel. "Grab some gear. We should spend a couple of days here before heading back." When they got back, they'd immediately request another trip. A bigger one, with more funding. This place would need protecting.

There'd be research papers, books, interviews, guest lectures...this was the kind of discovery that scientists dreamed of. Something that would make their name last forever. He basked in the imagined praise for a moment. Then his rope jerked, and he dropped enough that his toe of his boots just scraped the ledge.

"We should go up, not bringing them down," Brian muttered.

"I'm going to get some gear," Viv called.

"Bring more rope and anchors." They'd need more gear to get down to ground level.

The ledge was about the size of a single bed and it wasn't the only one. The cliff face was littered with ledges, some barely a toe hold, others were wide and long—enough for a small team of scientists to rest on. As long as the ledge he was about to drop onto didn't slide away, everything would be fine. He drew in a breath and held it as he released the rope. His feet hit the rock, and the rock held. He let go of the rope but didn't unclip.

"It's your fault we're down here," Brian said.

"I saved your life." It would've been easier to let go.

"You only had to save it because you wanted to go deeper. You're a cowboy."

And you're a coward.

"Look around. This is what we're here for." He wanted to get down there doing some actual field work. Too much of his time had been spent in a lab. He glanced at Brian who was still pressed up against the rock face.

"We need to go back up and tell the base where we are and what we've found."

"We can take a vote. We're still within the guidelines." But Saxon was willing to bet they'd be told to return, get a bigger team, and so on. They wouldn't be allowed to look around and be the first people to ever walk in an Antarctic forest.

"We don't know that it's safe. This your first trip—you don't know shit."

Saxon stared at him. "Can you not appreciate the wonder? We're in Antarctica." He swept his arm out. Not that he could tell from the weather and the greenery down here. There would be a blizzard outside, and they'd be toasty warm in this temperate slice of the south pole. "Why did you come if you hate being out in the field?"

"I enjoy being in the field...I just don't like caves and insects. The centipedes attacked me."

"Did they sting you?"

"No." Brian used a gloved hand to wipe his forehead. "How hot is it in here?"

"No idea, but you don't need that. Leave it up here and put it on when we go back up." Brian glared at him like Saxon had suggested he remove his skin. "You'll overheat with it on."

"We're ready to come down," Carmel called. "I've got the climbing gear."

"Wait...we need to discuss this," Brian called up.

The two women peered down, and Saxon hoped they were attached to something.

"I want to see the trees," Viv said.

"We need to report back. We can come down tomorrow," Brian argued.

"Or we can take a good look around, so we have something to say more than 'fell through a hole into a prehistoric forest,'" Carmel said. "All in favor of exploring?"

Viv agreed with Carmel. Brian crossed his arms and stared at Saxon.

Saxon lowered his gaze. As much as he wanted to explore, Brian had a point. But he'd also said no to everything. Instead of using his name to gain to further scientific research, he was doing nothing but playing it safe. Saxon lifted his gaze and held Brian's stare. "I say we explore."

Brian shook his head. "You'll never get on another field trip, kid."

"I'm not a kid." He'd been fighting his way up his whole life and he doubted that Brian had that much pull. "Besides, I found the centipedes."

Brian's lips twisted into a sneer. "That doesn't mean shit. You'll need to have your paper peer-reviewed and you're a no one. You'll need a co-author. Anything that comes out of this has all our names on it."

Saxon nodded. He knew that. "Guess we leave out the parts where you didn't want to do anything more than wander the upper tunnels."

Carmel landed between them. Breathless and smiling now, she was no longer fending off centipedes. Viv followed moments later. They secured a new anchor point and dropped a rope down to the ground.

Saxon couldn't help but smile. "I'll go down and find another ledge if it comes up short." He looked at Brian. "If that's okay?"

"Sure." But the word was as cold and slick as ice.

Saxon bounced down the cliff, aware he was the first person to ever set foot in the cavern. The rope fell short, but there was enough rock rubble that he was able to scramble down. The trees were stunted, with none over three meters, and their leaves were large and dark as if to make up for the lack of direct sun. They were cycads, ferns, and conifers. He was in a prehistoric forest.

A remnant from another time.

And he was the first human.

Carmel landed next to him. "Holy fuck."

"Yeah."

"Like really...this is...it's incredible." She let out a whoop. "We're going to be so famous."

Saxon nodded. They'd become experts in whatever they found. Give talks at prestigious universities and be given money to do more research. Everyone would want to be part of this. "Thank you for insisting I come."

How had he ever thought about declining the expedition?

But he knew why...his father had said he was chasing a dream. Doug had expected him to be waiting at home while he went away all the damn time. They all wanted something from him—no one asked what he wanted.

"You needed to be here…you're good in the cold, can climb, and you spent so much time in those frozen Tasmanian forests."

"So did you."

"That's why I knew this was your kind of thing. Because it was mine." She smiled.

And there'd been a time when he'd tried to want her because that would've been easy. They both knew better. "Are you sure you're okay?"

"Yeah." She shivered. "I don't know why I got so freaked."

"Because they're huge and unexpected?"

"Maybe." She gave him a tight smile. "Hopefully, there's not more of them down here."

There could be anything. It was exhilarating and terrifying and he felt like a kid on Christmas Eve. If he'd listened to his family and boyfriend, he wouldn't be here. "Doug didn't want me to come."

"Because he's the only one allowed to leave?"

Being in the Army meant Doug was often away. Most of the time that was fine. But he was tired of feeling like the relationship was little more than convenience. He fed the cat and watered the plants while Doug went off and lived his life.

How could he stay home when there was so much world to explore, and he had a chance to do something of note? Doug would have to find another solution. Maybe he'd need to find another boyfriend.

Brian landed heavily and stumbled down the rubble before landing on his knees. He stared at the dirt, rich and dark and made of decomposing leaves. "Where are we?"

"An ice cave…" A huge cavern beneath the Antarctic ice. They were in a dome that had preserved life as it had once been before Antarctica had frozen over.

"In a caldera, I think," Carmel said. She turned and glanced up as Viv made her way down.

"Look at these…the plants!" Viv landed, unclipped, walked straight up, and touched one. "Amazing."

Saxon stared at the trees. "If all these plants survived, what are the odds something else did?"

"Other than centipedes?" Viv asked with a grin.

"Yeah, other than centipedes." Something that Saxon would enjoy studying. Viv was the bug lover.

"I hope there's nothing out there," Brian said. "This place shouldn't exist. We shouldn't be here."

"This is exactly where we need to be. This is where science is done." Carmel picked up one of the bags.

Saxon nodded. "Let's make a plan. Find a place to camp. Take it in turns to sleep so we make the most of our twenty-four hours."

"We could do forty-eight and still make it out in time for collection," Carmel said. "It will be months…maybe not until next summer before we get to come back."

"Our camping gear is up there. Everything is up there." Brian pointed up at the hole.

"We have food and water and sample bags," Carmel said. "Enough for a day."

"Come on, Brian. You were saying how much you loved coming to Antarctica." Viv smiled and for a moment, Saxon thought Brian's mood would shift.

It didn't. Brian narrowed his eyes. "It's like being trapped with three copies of my ex-wife. Always pushing."

Viv stepped back, then spun away.

Brian's face twisted into a snarl, but he didn't say anything else.

Saxon gave him a glare. "We're supposed to work as a team. You can put in a complaint when we get back to base."

"I will. You'll never come here again. I'll make sure of that," Brian said.

"Yeah, because you know people," Carmel said. "I know people too. We all do."

Saxon didn't. Not really. He knew that he should make more of an effort to friend the right people, but that took the shine of the science. It should be about the work, not the connections.

He'd met plenty of people like Brian. They didn't care about anyone but themselves, but they did care what other people thought of them. They always wanted to be the top dog. The one that was looked up to. They claimed that like it was theirs by birthright, not through any work. Maybe Brian had been a good scientist once, but now he wanted easy praise.

Saxon glanced at the forest. "There's so much to document. We could spend a week here and not cover more than a few square meters."

Brian sighed. "You don't get it. You'll do all the hard work and someone else will walk away with it all."

"Your ex?" Saxon had heard enough about the ex-wife to figure out she'd put up with a lot of shit.

"The best you can do is go on trips and do just enough to justify the next one. Have some fun. Because at the end of the day, none of it matters."

Saxon shook his head. "You're wrong. This matters. This place could hold the answers about surviving dramatic climate shifts. About life itself. It's like we're standing in the past." Or on an alien planet. "We're the first people down here. Ever."

"And we aren't armed."

"What?" Carmel snapped her gaze to Brian.

Brian shrugged. "No one knows what's down here. We have cameras and sample bags for soil scrapings. We already know the centipedes aren't friendly."

"You disturbed their feeding, and they attacked," Carmel said. "If you don't want to explore, you stay here."

"All I'm saying is that we should be careful. We don't know where we are." Brian was still attached to the rope. "And I don't think we should split up."

Saxon sighed. If this was a slice of pre-historic forest, there could be anything down here. Giant wombats, thylacinids, something older? When had this bubble become trapped? Excitement at the possible discoveries gave his heart a flutter. "I agree with Brian. We don't know what's down here, so we should stay together."

"There won't be any big predators because there isn't enough land area to support big herbivores," Viv said. "No brontosaurs or tyrannosaurs." She laughed but the way she glanced at Saxon was like she wanted him to nod in agreement.

Which he did. He frowned, trying to remember what he'd learned about dinosaurs, while at the same time hoping that Viv was just having fun. "There were no tyrannosaurs this far south, but there were other theropods. And other herbivores."

"What are you saying?" Carmel asked.

Saxon shrugged. He didn't know. They hadn't even looked around to see if there were signs of animal life. "Nothing…but it would be cool if there were some dinosaurs."

Would they be anything they recognized or something different, smaller obviously because of Insular Dwarfism. But he doubted it. It was more likely there'd be other creatures, maybe small primitive mammals…although would they be primitive when they'd had centuries to develop?

Brian shook his head. "Are you five?"

"Well, what do you think is down here?"

"It doesn't matter what we think, it matters what we find and we won't do that standing here." Carmel glanced at Brian. "Shall we go?"

Brian needed no more cajoling. He unclipped and strode past Saxon and Carmel to suck up to Viv. Saxon shook his head.

Carmel rolled her eyes. "At least he's predictable."

An apology for dragging them all down formed, but Saxon swallowed it down. This was the discovery they'd come here to make.

They walked into the forest, pushing through the undergrowth. They gawped at the trees—some had trunks so thick all four of them wouldn't have been able to encircle it. How old were they? It would be a waste to cut one down to find out. When they found a fallen tree, they'd stopped to take measurements and photos and samples.

They were all taking photos, of leaves, of a pile of scat. Of claw marks... Saxon put his hand out as he took the photo. There were only two at hip height; he could run his first and second finger along the grooves in the bark.

Maybe it wasn't claw marks.

He glanced behind him. Every rustle of the leaves and the bushes now hid something.

Well, of course it would. They were in a forest. If he'd been in the wilds of Victoria or Tasmania, he would have said it was a snake or a lizard. That's probably all it was here too.

Even Brian seemed revived. And was far more competent than Saxon had thought. When he looked at Brian, he was reminded that if he stopped caring about the science and only cared about his ego, that's what he'd become. Saxon took a drink of water and pushed the sleeves up of his thermal top. They were overdressed down here.

Viv stood up from whatever she'd been looking at. There was so much here they were stopping every other step, strung out along the trail over several meters. "Did you hear something?"

All chat stopped. Saxon listened, but all he could hear was the thump of his heart and the whisper of leaves. There was no breeze down here, not enough for the leaves to rustle anyway. There was something in the bushes watching and following them. He slowly turned, taking in what was around them, but couldn't see any movement. Yet he was sure there were eyes on him. There was an invisible target was on his back.

"If there's something out there, it's probably wondering what the hell we are." He tried to make a joke, but it sounded forced even to his ears.

The laughter that followed was equally tight.

He regretted drinking so much water as he needed to pee, and he didn't want to be going behind a tree on his own. He glanced back the way they'd come where white chalk marked the trees so they wouldn't get lost. There was nothing on the path and anything here was probably more afraid of them.

"Brian, want to watch my back while I take a leak?"

Brian scowled, but if he complained, Saxon wouldn't watch his and he could see the calculations cross on the older man's face. He didn't want to have his back unguarded either. "Fine."

"We might do the same. Meet back here in a few minutes?" Viv brushed a lock of hair off her forehead.

With that, they went to trees on opposite sides. Saxon couldn't shake the feeling of being watched. The occasional sound that didn't quite fit. Of course there would be creatures here, small things. Reptile things, insect things, small mammals—hell, there were probably even rodents. That was all it was. They'd found insects under logs—the usual thing one expected in a forest. And the claw mark? He tucked himself away and studied his surrounds while doing the polite ignoring of Brian relieving himself.

"I think there's a trail over there." If there was a trail, it meant something had made it. But it also meant easier walking. He waited for Brian, not willing to cross the two meters to investigate on his own. This was ridiculous. One rustle and he was freaking out.

Brian finished and peered through the leaves. "You're right…if there are footprints, we might be able to work out what kind of animals live down here."

Together, they walked over. It was definitely a trail. Saxon squatted down at the edge to look at the myriad footprints. None of them looked familiar—no rats or possums. What had lived here when Antarctica had still been covered in forest? "This one looks like a bird."

"There's so many prints."

"It probably doesn't rain down here, so they never get washed away, just trampled over."

"So they could be fresh or centuries old." Brian took a few photos, carefully placing a scale next to each one.

"Or even millennia." He glanced up at the crystalline blue of the ice ceiling. It was hard to tell how deep they were, or how big the cavern was. When he climbed up, he'd need to get an estimate.

A shriek cut through the silence.

Something made chirping noises. Then the undergrowth was alive with noise and flashes of red. Saxon turned, trying to see what it was, but they were too quick and too well hidden by the shrubs. Saxon started back to the tree where they'd agreed to meet.

Brian grabbed his arm. "What are you doing?"

"Finding out what's going on." Carmel and Viv wouldn't scream without reason.

"You don't go toward danger."

Saxon shook off his grip. "We don't know it's danger."

Then someone screamed. A human cry of pain.

"It's got her! It's got Viv."

"We're coming." Saxon ran back to the fallen tree, Brian at his heels. "Where are you?"

"Up here," Carmel called. She was wedged in a tree as high as she could go. "They took her."

"Who took her?" Saxon glanced wildly around the clearing.

"Viv?" Brian shouted.

But the forest was silent again; not even the leaves whispered.

CHAPTER 3

Brian yelled as though he could summon Viv if he called her name enough times, while Saxon helped Carmel out of the tree. Carmel wasn't usually afraid of anything—giant centipedes excepted, but who wasn't creeped out by them?

"What did you see?" Saxon reached up a hand to her.

"Nothing." She grabbed his hand and jumped down. "Well, not nothing. I had my back turned, doing up my pants. I heard rustling and a weird clicky chirp. That was all. Then Viv screamed. I turned and saw her legs disappearing into the shrubs." Carmel pointed.

"And you climbed the tree?"

"No. I tried to grab her legs, to get her back. She was screaming. But one of them knocked me to the side." She shook her head. "It was like a *T-rex*."

It couldn't have been. "They're big. Too big to live here." But that didn't stop him from glancing around, expecting another attack.

"It was tiny. Hip high." She rubbed her arm and her fingers came away bloody. She lifted her gaze to stare at him. "It was definitely a dinosaur."

"Like a *Velociraptor*?"

She shook her head. "No big toe claw. Big eyes though and hands with claws."

If there were predators, she smelled like wounded prey. "Let's get the scratches patched up."

"We need to find Viv," Brian said. "Before they kill her."

"We don't know where they took her." Saxon didn't want to believe there were small theropods running around the forest. But at the same time, the idea of finding actual living dinosaurs sent a thrill through him. This was a proper, ancient lost world.

"Or why they took her." Carmel's voice still had a wobble. "Why didn't they kill us both on the spot?"

"You got lucky," Saxon said, hoping that was the truth.

"Leopards stash their prey," Brian said.

No one spoke as Saxon bandaged Carmel's arm. The dinosaurs, theropods, or whatever they were, took live prey. To stash? To feed to their young? Whatever it was, Viv hadn't screamed again.

He glanced around the area the women had chosen for a bathroom break. It was no different to where he and Brian had gone. They could've picked this side. Had the dinosaurs been following them, hunting and looking for the weakest? Why not the oldest? They'd never seen humans before, so how would they have even decided to take Viv? Or had it been pure chance?

The filtered blue light that had made the cavern seem enchanted on first entry now became oppressive, creating dark shadows everywhere Saxon looked. Anything could be out there. If there was one predator, there would be more, and they now knew that humans were easy prey.

Something chittered in the distance and Saxon shuddered. When another responded, he wanted to run. The primitive part of his brain had decided this whole idea was a bad one and they should head to the surface and come back when they were better prepared. But Viv was still out there…was she even alive? "What do we do?"

"We aren't leaving her," Brian said.

"I didn't say we were, but we don't know what we're dealing with or if…" He couldn't say it when Brian was staring at him like he was about to snap—whether that was tears or punching Saxon in the face, he wasn't sure.

"She was alive when they took her. We have to assume she's still alive," Brian said.

Saxon nodded. He didn't know which was worse—that Viv was alive while the dinosaurs prepared to eat her, or that she was dead and they were risking their lives going after her.

"We need to call for help," Brian continued. "Send someone up while the other two search for her."

"You were the one who thought splitting up was a bad idea. If we send one person back to the rope, they'll be an easy target." And if they started talking about dinosaurs, base would laugh at them. But the idea of running and getting out of here was appealing. Saxon glanced at Carmel.

Carmel pulled her bloody shirt sleeve down. "If we send someone up, and wait for base to fly someone in, by the time they get here, she'll definitely be dead. If we're going to rescue her, we do it now and we stay together."

"But if someone goes up, there'll be medical help waiting. I knew this was a bad idea. I told you we shouldn't be running around down here." Brian cut a glare at Saxon like it was his fault. If Brian hadn't fallen through the hole, none of them would be here. "Fine. We go after her while the trail is fresh. Move in fast and then get out of here." Brian put his hands on his hips, warming up to being in charge of the rescue.

"And when we find her, and find more of those things, what then?" Saxon looked at Carmel, hoping for back up. "We should all head up."

"I'm not leaving her and since we're staying together, you're staying with me."

Carmel looked at Brian, then Saxon. "If it were you who were taken, what would you want us to do?"

Saxon wanted to say that he'd expect them to run but couldn't. He'd want them to come after him and save him. "What are we dealing with?"

"It's some kind of raptor." She closed her eyes. "A little spikey, big hands and claws and big eyes."

Brian gave a nervous titter. "Good thing you don't have a basket of baked goods to take to granny."

Saxon glared at him. "How many?"

"I don't know. They struck fast. One second silence, a rustle, then there was screaming. Two, three…maybe more." She glanced around as if expecting to see another. She licked her lip. "I think we should give ourselves a few hours to find her, that's all. And if she's dead, we need to leave. Sorry, Brian, but I'm not going to drag her body out of here."

"Agreed." Brian's gaze kept flicking over the bushes. "Do you think she's alive?"

Carmel nodded.

It would be easier if Viv were dead. Then they could run. He was a selfish shit; not even Brian wanted to leave her.

"No getting close. If she's alive, we act smart and watch and plan," Brian said.

They needed more than a plan. "We need weapons."

If they'd had all their gear, they'd have had more to choose from. As it was, they only had small knives, heavy-duty torches, and ice picks. Not enough. He wished he had his flare gun. No one had brought theirs. They were carrying enough for a small excursion down one tunnel with the expectation of being back for dinner—they'd all packed enough food for a day though. This was no one's first field trip.

Going after Viv didn't seem like the smart thing to do as they pushed through the ferns where she'd been taken and broke onto the trail with clear drag marks. He flinched at every sound as he brought up the rear, heavy torch in one hand, ice pick in the other. Carmel and Brian carried the same. While he trusted Carmel, Saxon wasn't sure about Brian.

But Brian wasn't a total fool—he was still marking every third tree with a line of chalk—but he definitely had his own self-interest at heart. Who was playing the hero now?

Saxon's sense of direction was shattered. Every tree looked the same, and their canopy hid most of the ice dome. He didn't know if they were heading toward the edge of the caldera or the center. But he was aware of the stink of rotting vegetation and the way some plants didn't seem healthy. Was the air poisoned with volcanic fumes?

He inhaled but couldn't smell any sulfur. They were exploring with no idea what they were breathing in. Well, if the Red Riding Raptors were fine, then they would be too. He clung to that thought, knowing it was bullshit. There'd be viruses down here that had never had a human host.

Brian stopped and pointed. For one hopeful heartbeat, Saxon thought he'd found Viv, but it was a river. Only two meters wide, but a river with a current all the same, and on the other side were six little dinosaurs. They couldn't have been bigger than him, and they were definitely sauropods.

"It's like Gulliver's Travels Jurassic edition." Brian snorted at his own joke and the sauropods looked up.

"Cretaceous," Saxon corrected.

"What are you talking about?"

"Cretaceous came after Jurassic."

"And?" Brian glared at him.

"And, any Jurassic dinos would be extinct, replaced by their better-adapted cousins. Although…maybe these aren't even Cretaceous. Maybe they're more evolved." Millions of years cut off from the rest of the world. They wouldn't be in any textbook or museum.

"They'd have to be to survive down here. They've all got big eyes." Carmel pointed to the sauropods.

"Which means they can see better than us in the dim light." Saxon put down his pick and torch and took some photos. He was thankful they'd come during summer when it was light all day; in winter, this cavern would be trapped in perpetual night.

"Insular Dwarfism," Carmel said.

"Yeah, that too." They'd all gotten smaller to survive in the area they had. Not that being small made them any less dangerous. Standing by the river, anything could be watching them. He glanced up at the cavern roof and tried to see the walls to get his bearing. "We need to move on."

"Not getting a sample? Put one in your bag for later study?" Brian asked.

"There'll be another trip." And there'd be soldiers. They'd make a proper camp down here. A field lab. "We just need enough evidence to make it tempting to people with money— isn't that right?" Saxon threw Brian's words back at him. "I'm sure some of your friends would love to fund a trip into the Antarctic Cretaceous."

"Yeah, yeah. Probably." But Brian's gaze was on the ground, not the dinosaurs.

"Which way?" Carmel asked as she studied the riverbank.

There was slime on the edge of the bank and on the rocks. How deep did it go, and what was in there? It was too easy to imagine something in the depths now that there were actual dinosaurs watching him. This wasn't the discovery he'd wanted to make—but it would still rock everyone's world.

All they had to do was get Viv and get out.

A part of him wanted to turn and flee. She was probably already dead, and they would be soon too if they didn't leave. But he wanted to know what else was down here. A whole little world, in a frozen bubble. This place could keep his career going indefinitely. He'd become an actual dino biologist, no paleobiology or archaeology required.

He zoomed in on the sauropods on the other side of the river and took more photos. Then scanned their surroundings, looking for a clue.

"Get off me!" a woman shouted.

Saxon looked away from the camera.

"That was Viv," Brian said, already heading upstream like he knew where he was going.

Carmel looked at Saxon. "At least we knew she's alive."

But for how much longer? He looked away, knowing that he'd been thinking of leaving when she could be saved. Would they have left him? Who at home would have been gutted to hear of his death? His father would have no one to mock. He wanted to think Doug would care, but he wasn't sure. Three years and neither of them had discussed the future. Maybe they didn't have one, and they'd both remained for the convenience.

Would he have been so keen to leave if it had been Carmel that had been taken?

They followed the river, and again, Saxon was sure they were being followed. He saw dinosaurs the size of chickens but with fewer feathers digging in the ground with their clawed, winged, front limbs. They scattered when the human approached, disappearing under leaves to wait until the unknown creature had passed.

A herd of herbivores standing on two legs nibbling the delicate ends of ferns formed a protective circle around their young when they saw them. Saxon wanted to pause and take it all in. It was magic, and wondrous, and terrifying every time he saw something new and unexpected. He felt like a giant among the small dinosaurs, though he was glad the dinosaurs weren't the giants.

If the dinos were, they'd probably be dead already.

They'd been walking for close to an hour, following the river, when the ground started to rise. Saxon was no longer sure they were heading in the right direction. He had no idea where they were. Brian kept muttering about finding her.

Carmel was gathering anything she could, bagging it and putting it in her backpack.

"Brian, we're wandering blindly." Even though it hadn't gotten dark, it was long past dinner time and if they didn't rest, they wouldn't be able to keep going. "We need to stop and eat and think this through."

Brian rounded on him. "We have to get her before they eat her."

"I get that." As much as Saxon knew the longer they stayed, the bigger the risk, he also didn't want Viv to get eaten.

"Do you?" His eyes blazed.

"Saxon's right, we need to eat and work out where we are in relation to where we arrived. And we've lost the trail."

"Fine. We'll stop for thirty minutes. No more. We'll rest when we get out of here, with Viv."

They didn't light a fire, just ate some cold rations. Saxon ate half his chocolate bar and shoved the rest into an outer pocket in his backpack so he could access it later. His water bottle was almost empty and there was no ice to melt.

He was going to have to risk the river and a purification tablet. It was just glacier water, with dino spit and who knew what else? He walked over to the river and kneeled. The water was dark blue, reflecting the starless, sunless *sky* of the cavern. He couldn't see anything swimming in there and the water was moving swiftly.

He put his hand in, shocked that the water was warm, rather than icy, and filled his bottle. It was almost a surprise that nothing tried to eat him. He turned. Carmel was repacking her bag. Brian was nowhere to be seen. Not three meters away from Carmel was a raptor.

It wasn't moving, just watching. All big eyes and red crest. Red Riding Raptor indeed.

And for a few heartbeats, Saxon did the same. It had big arms and big hands tipped with claws for grabbing. It stood alert, balanced by its tail and muscled back legs. It might have only been hip high, but in would have been two meters long. It was beautiful in the way the most predators were. Perfectly constructed for hunting and killing and he couldn't look away.

It chittered. Carmel looked up. She scooted back on her ass and grabbed her torch.

All Saxon had was his water bottle. His ice pick was near his bag. They'd gotten complacent when they'd gotten tired and hungry.

The raptor cocked its head as though intrigued by Carmel and took a step forward. Maybe it was just curious and there was nothing to worry about. Wild animals didn't attack unless hungry or threatened. It huffed out a breath and clicked again.

Carmel clicked back. Her knuckles were white around the handle of the torch.

Saxon remained frozen. If he ran toward the raptor, would it run away or attack him? He didn't know enough about their behavior to make a good guess. He wasn't even sure the creature had seen him. Was that tale true, that if you didn't move a *T-rex* wouldn't be able to see you?

These raptors had such big eyes they probably didn't even realize it wasn't daylight in here. In winter, it would be night for months. He didn't want to imagine what being hunted in the dark by raptor would be like. Unless, maybe they hibernated, and they'd have been perfectly safe.

He risked easing his foot forward, not wanting to draw its attention but unable to just watch and wait. The raptor's eye moved as if noticing him, but otherwise, it kept its focus on Carmel.

Sniffing and creeping closer, Carmel scooted back again, edging toward the river and him. Saxon had the distinct impression that it was herding her…and him together.

Shit.

Cautiously, he glanced to his left and then right, looking for another one. But he couldn't see any others. Maybe there were more hiding in the shadows. Or maybe this one was alone.

This weird dance continued with Carmel getting closer and the raptor following. Its breath smelled like rotting meat and it limped as it walked. Old and injured and looking for an easy meal?

Saxon tried to keep calm by noting its features, anything that could be used later to work out what it might be. A blood and tissue sample would be amazing, but they had nothing to compare it to. Teeth and claws and bones would be better.

Carmel was now only two meters away, which made the raptor only three. Far too close. Would it be worth a swim in the river to get away? For all he knew, there was something toothy in there. It would be just his luck for leopard seals to know about this place and come here for a summer vacation when they got sick of ice.

"Hey, where did you go?" Brian called.

The raptor turned its head, a swivel like an owl so it could look over its own back. Carmel swung the torch at its head as she stood. The torch never connected. The raptor's mouth opened.

"No!" Saxon leaped for Carmel, but he was already too late.

The raptor's jaws closed around Carmel's arm with a sickening crunch. She screamed and stumbled back into Saxon. Blood gushed from the wound. He grabbed her arm, squeezing hard. Part of it was reflex, even though his brain was telling him there was no point and they were all dead.

And he was next.

The raptor swallowed her hand with a crunch and chirped. Then it lifted one of its legs and lashed out. The kick caught Carmel on the thigh. Blood bloomed and spread down the leg of her pants.

She kicked back, pushing against Saxon as she did. "You greedy fucker."

Saxon tried to drag her away. If they could get up a tree... He lost his grip on her arm or she pulled away. The raptor kicked again, opening another set of wounds. Her leg became instantly soaked with blood. She looked at Saxon. "Get out of here. Save yourself."

No, he couldn't leave her.

The raptor kicked again, then used its hands to grab her. Its claws pierced her flesh as if were soft butter. Blood streamed from the wounds and she screamed at it, bashing the raptors snout as though it were a shark and she stood a chance of fighting it off. It dragged her closer and shoved its snout into her belly.

Brian ran down the hill, an ice pick in each hand. He attacked the dinosaur, putting a pick through its cervical spine and another through its eye. It twitched a couple of times as though trying to fight back but it was already dead.

So was Carmel.

CHAPTER 4

Saxon stared at the blood staining Carmel's clothes, her skin, the ground, and the raptor's face. Then he realized there was spatter on him. His hands were red where he'd tried to stop the bleeding from her severed wrist. He tried to rub it off on his shirt. It couldn't all be hers. She couldn't be dead. He kneeled next to her and tried to find a pulse or feel her breath on his cheek. He couldn't look at the way her stomach was ripped open or the way her pants were crimson with her own blood.

His eyes were hot. They'd been friends for close to a decade. His whole adult life. She'd been the one person who saw through his father's charming mask to the asshole beneath. It was because of her that he was even here. She believed in him when no one else would and he'd been close to quitting.

"She's gone," Brian said.

Saxon closed his eyes and swallowed hard, trying to find some kind of response. He didn't want to admit out loud that Carmel was dead. He grasped her hand. It was still warm. Her eyes were still open, staring at the ice dome above them. How could she be dead?

He shifted his gaze to the raptor. It was also staring up at the ice with its one good eye. It had never seen the sun or the stars or the southern lights. It didn't know that there no other dinosaurs beyond this cavern. To it, this was life as normal—except some weird animals had invaded.

That's all Carmel, or any of them were—animals. Big, tasty mammals.

The raptor wasn't terrifying now that it was dead. Its skin was a mottled gray, with a few red splashes. He noted the features and knew he should move and photograph it. Its amber eye was the size of his fist, perfect for the low light. Its teeth were pointed and serrated on the inner curve—all the better for grabbing prey.

They knew the raptors communicated and could hunt as a pack. What else should he be noticing? What else would help him survive?

Brian gave the dead raptor a kick. "I might take some samples." He kneeled and cut off the claws.

Saxon lifted his gaze from the raptor. "Where the fuck were you?"

"When?" Brian didn't look up from his butchering.

"You left her alone."

"*You* went to get water. I needed to shit."

"You needed to shit. You couldn't have waited another minute for me to get back?"

"You're blaming me for this?" Brian stood, bloody raptor claws in hand.

Tension boiled in Saxon's chest. The blood dripped off Brian's fingers and onto the dirt. "You ruined a perfectly good specimen."

He shrugged. "We can't take it, it's too big."

"You didn't photograph or document it. You took no measurements. You...you chopped it up for trophies." This was all wrong. Everything about this trip was wrong.

"We need proof that we found dinosaurs."

"That's what photos and field notes are for."

Brian laughed. "The people with money don't want photos. They want something they can touch. We came to get samples. I have the samples."

"You didn't even want to be here. You were more interested in getting in Vivian's pants than doing any work." Saxon stood, careful not to look at Carmel. "If we'd left after they took Viv, Carmel would still be alive." And they'd be halfway to safety, babbling about raptors to their rescuers.

Yeah, he was blaming Brian. It was Brian's fault they'd gone looking for Viv—Saxon didn't want to acknowledge that it was also the right thing to do—and it was Brian's fault that Carmel had been left alone, allowing the lone raptor to feel brave enough to attack.

Now there was only two of them and a forest full of raptors.

"Viv is still alive. We heard her after she was taken. We're going to get her back," Brian said, as though sticking with the original plan was still the best idea.

"Like hell. We're leaving. They'll have eaten her by now." And if they hadn't, they'd add Brian and him to the menu. They weren't equipped for this. But the raptors were. They had the teeth and claws and would make a couple of kicks to take them out. All it took was one cut in the wrong place and they'd bleed out. With luck, they'd be unconscious before the first bite.

Carmel had been alert for the whole thing. She'd known she was dying. She'd told him to leave. Her advice had always been good.

"They haven't," Brian yelled. His face had turned a shade a purple that Saxon was familiar with when his father was about to cut loose on him. "You're a fucking sissy."

But Saxon didn't step back and try to smooth ruffled feathers the way he would've at home. "Me? You didn't want to explore the caves. You didn't give a shit about discoveries. I don't even know why you're here."

"Because my friends have the money." He gave Saxon a slick smile. "I can make or break careers."

"So stay home and fail students."

"That's not how it works. Money wants discoveries." He waved the severed claws. "A few new microbes would've been plenty. But you wanted more. It's your fault we're all down here."

"Mine? You're the one who ran from the centipedes and sent us through the hole. You're the one who wanted to go after Viv when we should have left. You really think she's still alive? You think she'll be so grateful to you that she's going to let a man old enough to be her father stick it to her?"

Brian yanked the ice pick out of the raptor's eye. It made a small sucking sound and fluid splattered on Saxon's pants. "Yes." Then as Brian started walking away, he paused. "We're getting Viv. If we split up, they'll pick us off. Be smart."

Saxon stared at the ice pick in the back of the raptor's neck then at Brian's back. He was right—if they split up, they were dead. The longer they stayed, the more likely they were dead.

"And what about Carmel?"

"She's dead, what does it matter?" Brian packed up as though he'd decided it was time to move on and expected Saxon to follow his orders.

Saxon glanced up at the ice sky. He wanted to be on the other side of the ice dome. "We can only share the discoveries if we're alive. We need to leave."

"We're getting Viv."

"You're going to risk your life to get her body but leave Carmel here?" He flung out his hand toward his dead friend. He needed to survive to tell her family. If they all died down here, would another team eventually find the cave?

Hundreds of years in the future, they'd find human bodies and dinosaurs and wonder what had gone on. He didn't want to be someone else's fascinating discovery.

"Viv is alive," Brian screamed. "Stop saying that she's dead."

"You're delusional. We're in a cave with raptors. They took her, and she's gone."

"Shut up. You should've stayed home waving your rainbow flag. You're only here because Carmel insisted. You're a no one. A nothing."

Saxon rocked back on his heals. "I may not have friends in high places, but my work is solid."

And he wasn't a foolish blow hard trying to attract a much younger girlfriend either. Except Brian had been all about protecting his own ass and doing as little as possible until Viv was taken. Brian wouldn't do that if it wasn't a sure thing.

And Viv had never pushed Brian away or disparaged him. She'd rolled her eyes but smiled at him. Carmel had said something about Viv being flattered by the attention. But it was more than that.

"You're already banging her. You weren't trying to impress her at all. How long have you been together?"

"That doesn't matter."

"It does since you're risking my life to find your girlfriend. Which came first, the invitation to explore or the sex? Did you seduce her with promises of glory? That's what you did, isn't it? You picked out a target and moved in. You're just shitty because another predator got in first."

Brian slipped his backpack on. "Hurry up and pack up. The quicker we find her, the quicker we get out of here."

Saxon tugged the pick out of the raptor's neck and trudged up the hill. He was still missing something. Brian wasn't the type of man who went out on a limb for anyone. Why was Viv so important?

Why was he such a shit, for wanting to run while he still could? If there was a chance Viv was alive, they should rescue her. He glanced back at Carmel, knowing that chance was small. But he wouldn't want to be the one left behind and facing death.

Small scavengers with soft quills darted in and out from under leaves and snatched scraps of flesh from Carmel's open gut.

He ran back down the hill. "Get away."

He stood guarding the body, not sure what to do. Carmel had told him to leave but leaving on his own would be deadly. Even now, they were probably being watched. He closed his eyes and drew in a breath, knowing he needed to get moving and join Brian in his foolish plan. Find Viv, dead or alive, then leave. But he wanted to bury the body so it wouldn't be eaten by scavengers—or would they just dig it up?

They didn't have shovels big enough for the job.

Or the time, food, or energy. They had enough for a day, maybe two. He willed his mind to find focus. He'd been caught out when hiking and climbing. He knew how predators behaved. He couldn't be the weakest or the one culled from the herd. Not that two was a herd.

They had to stop acting like prey.

How did one convince a raptor that they weren't prey? These raptors were the top of the food chain—had been for millennia—and they didn't know any better. They had probably never known fear.

Brian crossed his arms and stared down at him. "You're wasting time."

"I'm saying goodbye." Apologizing for not burying her or protecting her, he drew in a breath, knowing the best thing he could do now was leave. He stalked up the hill, went through Carmel's bag, and took everything that would be useful—food, water, tools, and her samples—and put it into his backpack and adjusted the straps.

From up here, he took a photo of the scene. Proof that what they said was true, no matter how unbelievable. He tried to view it like he would any carnivore kill. It still bothered him that there'd only been one this time, when the first attack had involved several.

Were they like lions with the females hunting together and the single males hunting alone? He remembered the limp; it was more likely the raptor was old and sick.

He stared at the dinosaur, not Carmel, but didn't know enough to make any guesses. Maybe it had just been hungry and seen an easy meal.

Every raptor in the cavern would know they were easy to hunt by now. "Do you even know where you're going?"

"We'll just follow the river."

And walk until they ran into a wall or raptors. They'd lost Viv's trail. Saxon shook his head. "We need a better plan than that. I'll climb up and see if there's anything."

"I'm not staying down here like dinner."

"Then you climb as well." Saxon didn't wait for Brian to agree or start climbing. He picked the tallest tree he could find and scaled it. The bark was rough under his palms, but the simple action of climbing calmed his mind. It was familiar, even if nothing else was, and it required all his focus. For a few breaths, his mind stopped churning with fear and worry. The excitement of the discoveries that could be made was long gone.

But knowledge that this discovery would mean something...would make Carmel's death mean something...pushed him on. The branches became small, and springy, barely strong enough to take his weight. He risked going up a little further, taking his weight on his arms and his feet, so that the load was spread. His head poked above the canopy.

For a moment, the alien beauty of the blue light filtering through the ice and the dark green leaves consumed him, before he remembered what waited in the shadows. He glanced toward the river; the small scavengers were all over the bodies now. His throat thickened, and he quickly looked away.

Above him, the icy layer that formed the sky was still eerily blue. But there was a dark spot near the cliff—the wall of the caldera if Carmel was right—the hole they'd fallen through only hours before. Maybe if he squinted, he could pretend he could see the ropes dangling down, waiting for them. He couldn't see them, but it was enough to knew they were there, and that he had a way out.

He tried to estimate the distance and thought it was maybe a couple of kilometers from where he perched. Not far, less than fifteen minutes of running if he were at home on the suburban streets.

But that was very different than running through primordial forest with raptors closing in. He wouldn't make it at a run; he'd have to be smarter. They shouldn't have strayed so deep into the forest, chasing Viv's trail.

Every so often, leaves would shake or a ripple would go through the forest, and Saxon could only assume that dinosaurs were moving and going about their life the way they always had.

"Can you see anything?" Brian called.

Saxon looked over at where Brian's voice had come from but couldn't see him. If he wasn't careful, he'd end up taking all the risks, while Brian took all the glory for himself. Saxon sighed. This would become Brian's discovery—he had the friends with money and influence. He'd be lucky to be listed as an assistant. Maybe Brian wasn't all bad—after all, he cared about Viv.

Saxon turned to look at the rest of the cavern, expecting more of the same. This was a tiny ecosystem, the fragments of something that had once been much bigger. That it existed at all was worthy of awe. And it would be more awe-inspiring if they were equipped for a safari with dangerous predators.

"Nothing." He frowned. "Wait." He wriggled one arm out of the strap, the branch beneath his left foot creaking ominously.

"What? Do you see her?"

"No." Or at least he wasn't sure. He thought he'd seen a flash of the bright blue Viv had been wearing, but he could've been wrong. He fished around, feeling for binoculars, but only found a camera. That would have to do.

Balancing, more precariously than before, the backpack over one shoulder, and one hand now holding the camera, Saxon zoomed in on what appeared to be a clearing. The area was glassy and there seemed to be fallen trees, but there was something there. He zoomed in as much as he could. Four sauropods nibble on trees. Nearby was the splash of blue. Viv.

She was lying down in the dirt, partially obscured by the branches of the trees.

He took some photos. Why was Viv with sauropods? Why hadn't she got up to leave if she was alive?

"And?"

"And I don't know." But he couldn't forget Brian's suggestion as to why the raptors had dragged Viv away. Leopards stored their prey. So did spiders. He looked again, this time searching for raptors, gray and red in the shadows.

Was Viv dead or injured or just too scared to move because she was being watched?

The branch beneath him jolted as it started to give way, so he didn't wait for it to snap. He climbed down, not sure he was glad to have his feet on the ground. He searched the shadows but saw nothing and heard nothing. No clicks and rustles, so for the moment, maybe they were safe. Safe-ish.

Brian dropped out of the tree next to him and Saxon handed over the camera. Brian flicked through the photos, a frown forming. Was he thinking she was dead, and they could leave? He was an awful person for even thinking that, but he wanted to live. If they didn't try, Brian would let everyone knew it was Saxon who'd left her to be eaten.

They'd been down here for hours, and there was no way Saxon was making camp the way they'd first planned. He wasn't sleeping until he was safely above this ancient hell.

Brian handed back the camera. "Let's go get her."

"You didn't think any of that was odd?"

He shrugged. "We're scientists. Let's investigate."

Saxon stared at him and was very tempted to head off on his own. Brian would be forced to go alone or follow. How far would he be able to lead Brian before he realized they weren't heading to Viv? But if she was alive...

"How can we rescue her when we aren't even armed?"

Brian swung his ice pick. "Come on. They're only the size of a rottweiler. You've done work with Tassie Devils."

Yeah...which made him more wary of any predator. That and he'd never been a dog person. Cats were cool, and they knew exactly how to get what they wanted.

"Fine." He should make a video diary and leave the camera hanging in a tree so that when this place was discovered again, they'd at least have left something more than bones behind.

Assuming the new explorers were better prepared than they were. People would look for them when they didn't come back. The idea of having another team discover this place unprepared made him shudder. No one would be expecting dinosaurs.

"Lead on," Brian said with a wave of his hand.

"I'm going to have to keep climbing to check direction." Until they broke out of the trees, it would be impossible to go in a straight line, and following the river would take them too far away and leave them too exposed. At least in the forest there was some protection.

"And don't even think about misleading me." The ice pick was held too casually in Brian's hand, the end still bloodied. He hadn't hesitated. Saxon lifted gaze and Brian smiled.

Now he had to worry about raptors and Brian at his back.

With every step along the trial, all Saxon could think about was how he should've, somehow, pulled himself and Brian back up through the hole instead of going "wow, plants beneath the ice, let's have a look," like some kind of idiot.

No one had thought of the dangers—except Brian.

And no one had expected this.

Rustling to his left made him stop, ice pick gripped hard. He kept his gaze at large dog height. The leaves shook. He should've climbed a tree, not freeze, but it was too late to move as it was almost upon him. Then something size of a wombat bolted across the trail in front of him. Its clubbed tail disappeared into the shrubs. Another followed, along with several smaller ones. Babies. Finally, two medium-sized, armor-plated dinos crossed his path.

Brian swore. "What the hell was that?"

"Some kind of *Ankylosaurus*." Like most kids, he'd gone through a dino phase and he remembered enough to know his ceratopsians from his theropods, but that was about all.

"This place is a lost Cretaceous world. This will make me so rich."

"*Us* so rich." He didn't care about the money, but the accolades and the research that would be connected to his name. He wanted people to know who he was and what he'd done.

"Yeah. Yeah."

Nah. Brian was only thinking of himself. "We have to live for this to be worth anything. Otherwise, we'll be noted down as another lost Antarctic expedition."

"If we go back without Viv, you can forget ever working as anything other than a janitor in a lab again."

Saxon turned to face Brian. "What do you mean?"

"Vivian is one of *those* Anstruthers." Brian paused and smiled as if expecting Saxon to commend him.

Instead, Saxon stepped back. "You're dating one of the Anstruthers?"

That smug smile. "I traded up."

Saxon struggled to keep his face in neutral. "And why is Viv Anstruther dating you?" It was a common enough surname that he had thought nothing of it. Viv hadn't mentioned her family money—money made off research that then generated more money and research in an ever-growing positive feedback loop.

While Brian was fit and had a long list of achievements, he wasn't a catch for anyone under the age of thirty-five—but then Saxon really had no idea what straight women looked for in a man. Maybe there was more to Brian than his past glories and papers—though they had been enough for Saxon to want to be part of this trip.

"What kind of question is that?"

Saxon shrugged as though it didn't mean anything. "She's young and rich…"

"And dumb. So fucking dumb her parents bought her degree."

Brian didn't realize it, but her parents had bought him too. They wanted Viv's name on his research to continue their legacy. This time, Saxon was smart enough to keep his mouth shut. "Guess we should hope that she's alive."

"I was…what were you hoping?"

"To get out of here." Saxon started walking, knowing that no matter what happened he would get fucked over. This trip had been a jaunt for Viv to get her name on a paper or two and a business deal for Brian with a side of banging.

He and Carmel had been invited for legitimacy.

He shouldn't have pushed to explore deeper. He should've listened to Brian who been in the caves before and found just enough to tantalize his previous sponsors. This was never intended to be an in-depth field trip the way he and Carmel had been led to believe. Brian had raptor claws that he'd hand over to the Anstruthers and they'd make sure that only their pet scientists got a look. He'd never be coming back. He wasn't sure if that was a good thing or not.

"So what's your plan?" He kept his voice light, as though making casual conversation.

"Plan?" Brian asked, his footsteps heavy behind Saxon.

"When we get there? How are we going to get Viv to the ropes while being chased by raptors? They won't want to give up their meal." You didn't take a bone from a wild animal without expecting to get bit, and if Brian thought Saxon would sacrifice himself, he was dead wrong.

Viv Anstruther…returning without her would be the end of both their careers. He wasn't sure taking her body back would be much better. Unless Viv was alive, neither of them was getting near a lab again.

He kept thinking of the photos he'd taken. The fallen trees on the grass and the sauropods and Viv on the other side.

They walked in silence for what felt like hours, but was only minutes, before Brian finally answered. "There were no raptors around her. Maybe they left her alone and we can just get her and go."

"The dead don't run away. We're fucked no matter what we do." Saxon spun to face Brian. His eyes widened and the rest of his words died on his tongue. Not two meters behind Brian was a raptor. Their eyes met and Saxon couldn't pretend that he hadn't seen it. The raptor blinked.

Brian blanched. "Fuck...there's one behind me, isn't there?"

"Yeah." Better it was now, instead of in an hour or three. The waiting was over.

Brian clenched the ice pick.

The raptor didn't move, but it clicked once. A large leaf on the other side fluttered, and another raptor appeared.

Saxon chest ached with each breath like he'd been running. He should have led Brian back to the ropes and the hole in the ice. Hell, he should've taken off on his own. He could have gotten off the ground and climbed through the trees.

The raptors didn't move.

Brian glanced sideways. "You take one and I take one?"

"No...they're just watching us." Their large amber eyes tracked every movement. "Let's keep walking." He took a step back and then another. For all he knew, there was another behind him that Brian wasn't warning him about. But no bite came.

Brian walked toward him, his knuckles white and his nostrils flaring with each breath. "And?"

"And they're following." No closer and no more distant.

"What does that mean?"

"How the fuck should I know?" But he did. He'd grown up on a farm and seen sheep dogs in action. They were being herded. And when they reached their destination?

If they were going to fight, it would have to be before then. For the moment, he turned, walking forward as fast as he could. Going slowly and being careful didn't matter now.

He tried to do the math on how big the cavern was and how many apex predators the area could support. Did they eat a big meal every few days to once a week? Scavenge when they could? If the population was small, it would be too inbred to function…

The science kept him from falling apart but the panic stalked him, and he knew he couldn't escape.

"Can you stop running?" Brian panted.

Saxon hadn't even realized he'd been jogging. He stopped and noticed the raptors stopping too. "What are we going to do?"

"I don't know. But when we reach Viv, there'll be three of us against them."

Saxon groaned at Brian's eternal optimism. "And if she's dead, what then? Will her family muddy your name? Will you be blamed? How will you write up this misadventure? Assuming we get the chance."

The bitterly cold surface was a world away. As unreachable as the moon in a rowboat. But they were closer to the opening and their ropes to freedom than they had been when they'd been following the river.

One of the raptors clicked as though impatient.

"She's not dead," Brian said as though he could make it true.

Saxon started jogging again. Fuck Brian. Fuck the raptors. "You keep telling yourself that."

"We can't leave her down here."

"We left Carmel."

"That's different."

"Because she didn't have money?" There was a fork in the tracks. A raptor shot out onto the right-hand path, blocking their way. Saxon turned left like an obedient sheep.

"I think they're herding us."

Saxon didn't bother to answer. The trees were thinning, they were almost there, and they still had no plan with three raptors breathing their meaty breath down the back of their necks. He was running toward death and he couldn't stop.

CHAPTER 5

The leaves no longer brushed his legs, and the raptors weren't bothering about remaining hidden. They were slick, dark shadows that stalked them. Brian was breathing hard as they reached the edge of the tree line. Saxon had made his plan, and it involved getting up a tree and telling Brian to be the hero.

But he hesitated when he saw where they were going.

What he'd thought were fallen trees and branches from a distance weren't. He was ten meters away and saw it was a tangle of branches and bones that had never had the chance to be bleached. He was staring at a primitive fence. A corral.

They weren't just being herded—they were being penned.

"Oh shit." The words were little more than a sigh as he tried to catch his breath. The sauropods on the other side looked over the fence and bellowed. A family of sauropods…a breeding pair.

Saxon glanced at Brian. The raptors had culled Viv but not Carmel for a reason. They knew who the couple was. That meant he was expendable. His gaze slid to the raptors. They bounced from foot to foot like dogs waiting for the game to begin. Their large eyes watched him and Brian, and their nostrils flared. They clicked and chirped to each other.

"Viv!" Brian shouted, stepping next to Saxon.

Saxon put a hand on him. "Wait a moment."

"Viv, we're here. Give us a sign if you can."

"If we run out there, they'll chase us. They want us to run." Not a total lie but he didn't see any reason to let Brian know what he was thinking. He might be wrong.

He hoped he was wrong.

It wasn't like there was a body of research he could draw on and as far as he knew, no other predator penned their prey. Farmed their prey. He swallowed and swallowed again, his mouth dry.

Then he pulled out what was left of his chocolate bar, took a bite, and then tossed it toward the closest raptor. They weren't stupid, and he'd just proven it was edible.

"I'm scouting." Then he was up the nearest tree, pulling his legs up as fast as he could. A raptor snapped at his heels but missed.

"You lazy shit," Brian cursed him, but Saxon didn't care.

He climbed higher until he could see through the leaves. Viv was standing. "She's alive."

"Really?"

"Yes."

And the raptors hadn't attacked Brian, confirming his suspicions. His odds of survival dropped to something much closer to zero. Although, given the choice between being farmed by the local raptors and death, it wasn't much of a choice.

While up the tree, he went through his bag, looking for anything that might be useful. He had more food, but he didn't want to waste it…on the other hand, he didn't know why he was saving it. He shoved the small knife into his pocket. He had the pick and a torch which could be a club…he looked at the luminous blue twilight.

It was softly lit to him, but to the raptors, this was full daylight.

"Hurry up, our friends are getting twitchy." Brian's voice was higher than normal.

Saxon glanced down and all three were much closer to Brian. They wanted him in the pen with Viv. If Brian got into the pen, it would be much harder to get out.

Viv was alive and they couldn't leave her. And they couldn't join her. So they had to act now and then somehow reach the ropes without getting eaten. His plan wasn't going to get them that far. "I have an idea."

"What?"

"We'll blind them with the torches." Saying it out loud didn't make the idea turn into a plan. It was a temporary advantage at best.

"That's your idea?"

"You got a better one?"

"No." Brian shrugged out of his bag, which immediately drew the attention of one of the raptors.

"And give them your chocolate if you have any."

"Like fuck."

"Suit yourself, but if it distracts them…"

Brian pulled out the chocolate. "I'm going to scatter it then we'll turn on the torches so they can't see us, and we'll run and get Viv."

"Yeah." It still wasn't a plan, and Saxon would rather stay up the tree.

"And if they attack, I'll put a pick through their skull."

Saxon closed his eyes. Every raptor they killed was destroying the fragile balance that had existed here for millennia. The raptors were evolving, farming. It thrilled and terrified him. But what choice did they have?

"Wait, I'm going to signal Viv." He stood on the branch, and it flexed beneath his feet, then he turned on his torch, pointing it up so she could see the light and hopefully figure out what they were planning. "We're coming, be ready."

"I am." Her voice was strained.

He climbed down as low as he dared. A raptor jumped and snapped at him, barely missing. It landed and stared up at him. He unwrapped another chocolate bar and broke it up, stealing a piece for himself. It wasn't a great last meal, but it wasn't all bad either.

The raptor's nostril twitched, and its mouth opened as if it knew exactly what Saxon held in his hand.

"Are you ready?" he called down to Brian.

"You're faster."

"She's your girlfriend."

Brian muttered several unflattering things about Saxon and started to scatter the chocolate.

Saxon did the same with the uncharitable prayer, "I hope it makes you sick."

While the raptors squabbled over chocolate, Brian ran toward Viv and the pen. Saxon turned on his torch and aimed at the raptors' eyes. They stumbled and squinted. Their eyes that were so good in the endless dusk of the cavern that they couldn't cope with the bright light. And for the first time since realizing he was dinner, hope flickered.

Then the raptors turned their backs. No matter what he did, he couldn't get the light in their eyes without getting down. The one at the base of the tree didn't look up, but it was definitely keeping guard.

Saxon climbed back up to see what was going on. "Hurry up."

Viv climbed over the barrier, one arm held close to her body. A raptor ran toward them, one he hadn't seen. One that hadn't been following them.

"Behind you," he shouted.

He glanced down. The three near him were talking with clicks and chirps—it was definitely communicating, planning—then two bolted into the clearing after Brian and Viv.

The one below Saxon paced and scratched at the ground as though pissed at being left out of the fun. Then it looked up and chittered at him.

He would have to kill it. There was only one. He could do it. He had a torch and an ice pick. But the more it looked at him, the less he could. It was just an animal, doing what carnivores did—eat easy to catch things.

He had to be harder to catch.

He flicked on the torch and shone it in the raptor's eyes. It startled and flinched away. He used those seconds to make it across to the next tree, and then another. But the raptor followed, always just beneath him. He could clamber through the forest all day, but he'd still have to run for the ropes.

Viv and Brian yelled, calling for his help. He needed to help them; he wanted to run. But running on his own was pointless. He needed to get away from his guard.

He drew in a breath and dropped the chocolate wrapper. It fluttered to the ground, and the raptor fell for it. Saxon slithered down the tree, torch on, and as soon as the raptor looked at him, he shone the light in its eyes. It closed them and Saxon ran. He was tugged back as his backpack caught. He landed on the ground, the raptor far too close. It lifted its foot, and he rolled away, coming to his knees, face to face with too much teeth and fetid breath.

He lifted the torch, and the raptor turned, slamming its tail into Saxon's arm. He dropped the torch. He swung the ice pick, and the raptor leaped back, giving him half a second to grab the torch. Slowly he stood, holding his weapons, waiting for the next attack.

He took a step back and another, not daring to glance behind.

The one in front of him tilted its head then kicked at him, its claws barely missed him. Saxon shone the torch at it, but it closed its eyes and attacked anyway. He couldn't keep this up. Instead of going straight back, he sidestepped and swung the torch into the side of the raptor's head. It stumbled. And he did it again.

It bit the torch and wrested it out of his grip.

Saxon swung the pick into the raptor's eye. It connected like he'd stabbed an orange. Eyeball fluid squirted on his hand, and the raptor pulled away, taking the pick with it but dropping the torch. He grabbed it but collected a tail to the side of the head for his trouble. He staggered, not wanting to stay down, but tripped.

The raptor was on him. Its jaws right above his stomach, he shoved the torch into its mouth and pulled his pick free. The raptor gagged. His hand was slick with saliva, the other with blood and ocular fluid. Its teeth scraped his arm, and he forced it deeper and stood. Then he yanked his hand and torch free.

With a squeal, the raptor broke and ran into the forest.

"Yeah, you tell your friends I'm dangerous." He'd either scared away it or made an enemy.

He panted and dripped blood on the forest floor. He watched blood roll over his skin and drip off the end of his fingers. He wiped the back of his hand on his pants. The blood rivulets filled again.

He frowned. That wasn't good.

"Saxon," Brian yelled.

Saxon turned toward the noise. He was at the edge of the forest now, just grass between him and the pen where Viv and Brian were being herded. Four raptors were snapping and chirping and running and doing an excellent job.

If he ran, how far would he get?

The raptors were distracted with Viv and Brian. They had what they wanted, and he was expendable. A spare at best, and a snack at worst. He glanced up at the ice sky and toward the dark hole and safety. He might make it on his own, run as far as he could. If one followed, he could take it.

For a few breaths, he almost believed he could make it on his own. And when he crawled out of the cave and into daylight and called for help, would he lie and say the raptors ate everyone else or would he admit to leaving them to die?

How would he explain the raptors at all? They'd call it shock. Medicate him and put him on the ship back to Hobart.

A drugged bliss where he could forget. Until he was forced to remember.

The yelling washed over him, drowning the happy fantasy.

The cops would probably charge him with murder. Viv's family would demand answers and punishment.

And he'd never sleep again knowing that he'd left Viv and Brian to die here.

He wasn't sure he'd ever sleep again anyway.

They were all in this together until they made it out or died trying. He was betting on the later. He wouldn't ever get to write the research papers and become the first dino biologist.

If anyone remembered his name, it would be as part of the missing team. His parents would add it to the list of things he'd failed at. If he'd stayed in the family scrap business, none of this would've happened. Doug would be upset; he'd need to find a new lover to stay home and feed his cat.

That wasn't fair; they'd had good times. He'd always hoped it would become more. But he was done with waiting for other people to give him permission to get on with his life.

He stepped out from the scant protection of the shadows. "Stop yelling and running."

They were acting like scared prey. Brian should know better. The raptors swung their gaze at him and sniffed. Could they smell the blood of the friend on his clothes?

"Yeah, that's right, fuckers, I fought off one of you." Or were they just smelling his fresh blood? "Where's your torch, Brian? And the pick?"

"There's too many."

There was, and there was God knew how many more in the prehistoric forest behind him. He was tempted to glance over his shoulder but resisted.

"Treat them like sheep dogs. Smart but rabid sheep dogs." Who'd also become the farmer. "Don't run, move to your right."

Saxon went to his left, skirting the trees. His gaze flicking between the raptors, Brian and Viv and the pen.

The raptors didn't like it. They moved in closer, forcing Brian and Viv to go where the raptors wanted.

"You're going to blind them with the torch and make a break for it. Get up a tree."

There were four meters between Brian and Viv and Saxon. Behind Saxon were trees, and up them safety. But now the raptors had their prize, their pair, and they didn't want to let them go.

They used their tails and heads to nudge the humans back toward the corral. "Hold your ground."

If Viv and Brian got in the pen, it would be over. They'd starve to death or be slowly eaten. The raptors wouldn't be able to farm them the way they did the sauropods because humans didn't lay clutches of eggs. Bile rose in the back of his throat. He didn't know if Brian was listening. Viv clung close to his side.

Every conversation he'd had with her had been a lie. She'd been banging Brian the whole time. They'd both pretended that there was nothing going on. They deserved each other.

No one deserved this.

"You're going backward."

"I know. You're not helping."

And the longer Saxon stood there, the more exposed he felt. Like he was waiting to be attacked. This time, he couldn't resist, and he looked over both shoulders, but there was nothing in the shadows that he could see. However, he edged closer to a fat tree that looked easily climbable. "What would you like me to do? Lead an attack?"

"Do something," Viv said.

"I told you. Use the torch to blind them, then use the pick. Go for the eyes." He turned on his torch and kept the beam pointed at the ground. "Ready?"

Brian turned on his torch and aimed the light at the raptor by his side, and as expected, it shied away.

Saxon targeted the one at the front. "It won't last long."

They'd just close their eyes and hunt by scent, but he didn't say that. Viv and Brian had to believe they had a chance. While Brian distracted them, Viv bolted. She hadn't seen the raptors in action. She didn't know, or maybe her terror meant that she didn't care. She'd come too close to being eaten once and would do anything to avoid it again.

The lead raptor closed its eyes and gave chase, closing the distance in bounding steps. Saxon stepped forward and smashed the torch over the thing's nose. It ricocheted back and opened its eyes, only to get the full beam of the torch in its face. It hopped back, alternating between closing its eyes and sniffing and trying to open them.

Viv shot past Saxon.

"Get up a tree," he ordered. Running blindly would only get them lost.

Brian swung his pick and torch, but the raptors closed their eyes and used their tails. Brian fell.

The raptor in front of Saxon got brave and kicked, its long claws slicing the air as Saxon leaped back. A kick from a raptor would be worse than a kangaroo. He'd be gutted and dead within minutes.

Brian made a sound that should never leave human lips. A howl of pain. A raptor lifted its head, Brian's arm in its mouth.

Fuck.

He couldn't even see Brian under the swarm of raptors. The one in front of Saxon gave a final blind kick then ran to the feast.

Brian kept screaming.

"Oh God, help him," Viv cried.

What could he do? Brian was dead, he just hadn't realized. A raptor pulled out a slick sausage of intestines and ran, the glistening insides unraveled over the dirt. Another joined in the fun.

Saxon stood frozen, knowing that he needed to move, but unable to take a step.

He should've listened to Brian. Kept this a well-funded jaunt instead of trying to make a name for himself.

The screams became whimpers. How was he still alive? But the raptors were taking their time with delicate bites, tugging at his innards.

Viv sobbed behind him.

One of the raptors lifted its head as it chewed on a piece of pale intestine. The sausage flopped a few times before being swallowed. Saxon's stomach heaved, but there was nothing to come out.

He stepped back. "We need to go now."

"Nooo. We can't leave him." Her face was streaked with tears. She sat on a branch that was within chomping height and held her arm tight to her body.

"Do you want to be herded up and put back in the pen until they decide to eat us too?"

She shook her head.

"Then let's put some distance between us and them."

And pray.

But Saxon was sure that if there was a god, he'd forgotten about this place.

CHAPTER 6

The raptors didn't give chase. No matter how many times Saxon checked over his shoulder, he and Viv were on their own. Or at least it appeared that way. Every time he blinked, he saw Brian on the ground, the raptors slowly pulling him apart as if his groans added flavor.

Saxon hoped Brian was now dead.

"I can't." Viv stopped and clutched her side with her good hand. "You're bleeding and my arm is broken. We need to stop."

"We can't." But he was leaving a trail of blood that even the dumbest predator could follow, and the little raptors weren't dumb. He shivered, and his stomach went to water again.

They were dead; they were only running because it gave them something to do.

"Please. I need water and food. A sling," she pleaded. Her eyes were wide and sad, her face pinched and grimy.

She was right, but he didn't want to stop. He had to get them out of this.

"I want to get to the ropes. If we can get up high, then we can rest."

"So do I. Just a few minutes. Please."

How long until the raptors came looking for them? Minutes could make all the difference. That could be all the raptors needed to catch up with them. The forest was silent. In the distance, he could hear animals—dinosaurs—calling to each other, but not of the chittering and chirping that the raptors made.

With a look at her pained face he knew they wouldn't get far anyway.

He sighed. There was no point in dying hungry and exhausted. "We can rest up a tree when we find a suitable one."

Maybe Viv could tell him about her observations, and they could make an actual plan.

They walked a little farther. He'd been trying to skirt the forest, figuring it would be easier walking, and they'd be less likely to get lost, but it was also the long way. Maybe they should've cut through.

They found a big tree, and he helped her up, so they could rest above raptor jumping height. He handed her the torch and pick and flexed his fingers. They'd been locked in position for so long it hurt to stretch them.

"They're teeth marks..." she pointed at the bright yellow casing on the torch.

"Yeah." He pulled the first-aid kit out of the backpack. It hadn't been designed for dino-related emergencies. He pulled out the cloth that could be a bandage or a sling and left bloody fingerprints on it as he handed it to her. "I'll clean up a bit then help you."

He used an antiseptic wipe on the scratches on his hand and arm. There was another on his thigh and his pants were ripped, but the twin cuts were shallow. He covered the worst on his arm and hand with Band-Aids. The cuts were still bleeding, but there wasn't much else he could do.

What he needed was a tranq gun.

There was a bottle of painkillers. He shook it. "Want a couple?"

He wanted a bottle of vodka to wash them down.

All he had was half a bottle of tepid water. He took two and a drink then handed them over. "How's your arm?"

She shook her head and touched her upper arm. "I felt it crack when they dragged me away. It needs set, and I'm pretty sure it's not a good break. How am I going to climb up?"

"Easy. Once you're in the harness, I'll be able to pull you up as I climb. You aren't the first injured climber I've helped." He smiled like that was the least of their problems. If they were halfway up the cliff, he didn't care if it took them another day to get the rest of the way. They just had to get there and get off the ground.

He fiddled with the bloody wipes, wondering if he should drop them for raptor distraction or do the right thing and bag them up and take all their rubbish? "Why do you think they took you?"

"I don't know."

"They'd built a pen."

"I know. They had other animals in there. I saw one raptor bring food." She shuddered. "They licked me, tasted my blood. I thought I was going to die. Then they left me. And I lay there, pretending I was dead. This is a nightmare I'm going to wake up from," she said with such certainty that he wanted to believe her.

"Sure." He rummaged through the bag for more food and came up with some protein bars. Their cooking gear was all up top. He handed one over and did a quick check of their surroundings, but saw no raptors, though that didn't mean they weren't watching. "Have you been dating Brian long?"

She focused on unwrapping her bar. He should've done that for her. "Six months. I didn't want anyone to know…not until his divorce was final. Imagine how it would look, an affair, and then this trip. Everyone would think I'd slept my way up." She snorted. "They already think my parents smoothed my way with their money."

"Did they?"

"Why do you think I wanted to be here? They can't influence anyone in the field." Her eyes glassed up. "I wish I could call them and get their chopper in here. They could get a team in to rescue us." She sniffed. "And now it doesn't matter. Brian's dead. None of the plans we made will matter." Her hand lightly swept over her stomach.

Was she pregnant? Or had they just talked about it? He couldn't bring himself to ask. The raptors' desire for the two humans that were sleeping together was something he kept to himself. She didn't need to worry.

And now it was just the two of them. Would the raptors be happy with that?

He'd rather die.

"We should get moving." Sitting in the tree was an illusion of safety that he wasn't willing to dwell in.

"What's the plan?"

"To get out of here." He'd thought that was obvious.

"No, for when they attack." She lifted the torch and pick. "Is this all we have?"

He nodded. It had been working so far, but he knew that had more to do with luck and surprise than anything else. "We didn't come equipped for this kind of thing. We're scientists, not soldiers."

"We need to think like soldiers, or we won't make it."

He wished Doug was here. He'd come up with a plan to fight them off and get them to safety. Doug wouldn't have started exploring without being better prepared. "I left my soldier at home, but I have a penknife in my pocket."

"Well, that changes everything." She pressed her lips together. "I don't think they're following us because they know where we're going."

"That's not possible."

"Yeah? Yesterday, I'd have said meeting a dinosaur was impossible, yet today I found out they built pens to keep their prey in."

"That could just be this lot, some kind of adaptation." But maybe all raptors had farmed prey and there was just no remains of those farms. What else didn't they know because there was no fossil record?

"To not having enough prey?" She lifted an eyebrow.

"Maybe." If this ecosystem collapsed, he wouldn't be sad. Yes, he would be. It should be studied even as it failed. It should probably be saved. "But we are the prey at the moment."

"So we have to become harder to catch and kill."

Predators went after the easy targets, usually. The old, the weak, the sick. Humans didn't have armor plating or size. They were soft and noisy and that was about it. But they'd managed to kill one raptor and wound another...and the raptors had managed to kill two of them.

"They don't like light, but that's all we have. We didn't pack any weapons."

"Flare gun?"

He pointed up.

"Fire?"

Saxon frowned. "Our cooking stuff is also up there."

He doubted the raptors could be distracted with a nice ready to eat meal, even if they did like chocolate.

"Do you have matches or a lighter?"

"I don't want to burn this place down." The ice above would melt and collapse and bring down whatever was over it. It would be a disaster. He didn't want to be the kind of explorer that found something and obliterated it. Or the kind that was found dead a hundred years later.

Viv shook her head. "While I was lying there, I had time to think about how weird this place is. These animals have never seen fire. Ever. There's no lightning strikes down here. No storms. No nothing. We have that advantage."

"If they've never seen it, and haven't for millennia, will they still be afraid of it?"

"I don't know. We're the scientists though, so we should find out." She forced a smile, and he returned it.

"How's your arm feeling?"

"The painkillers didn't numb it nearly enough." She glanced down. "I should've helped Brian fight them off. Now he's..." Her voice broke.

"Then you'd either be dead, or in the pen wishing you were dead."

"And then what would you have done?"

"What do you mean? If they'd put you back in the pen?" Saxon swung his legs and watched a beetle crawl up the trunk. He wanted to say that he'd have tried again to set them free but couldn't. "I'd have left you and tried to reach the surface to raise the alarm."

"Why didn't you and Brian do that anyway?"

"Because he insisted that we get you." He lifted his gaze. "That we couldn't leave you because your family funded the trip." He needed to hear it from her if that was the truth.

"Oh…that's true. I'd always wanted to come here. Then when I met Brian, everything seemed to come together. I thought I'd found someone who cared about me and my work, not my family money."

Saxon wasn't sure Brian really cared about anyone but himself, but Viv didn't need to hear that while they were hiding up a tree from raptors. "He did care about you."

"Yeah…but not about my career. Only his. You probably think I'm stupid for dating a married man."

Saxon shook his head. "We all make mistakes."

She sighed. "I only realized when we were on the ship what a mistake I'd made. He'd known who I was from the start, and who my family was, before we started dating. The whole thing was a lie so he could be here."

"You mean your family funded it because of you, not him?"

"Of course. I've always wanted to come, so I started making it happen. When I heard that people were looking into the caves and theorizing about warm pockets, I was fascinated. I put together a proposal and got it approved. When no one has to find any funding, it's amazing what can happen."

"Are you still glad you came?"

Viv nodded. "Yeah. I found a lost world and saw the truth about my boyfriend. You can't buy those things."

"True." But the price had been in blood.

"What about you?"

He shrugged. They weren't out yet. There was still plenty of time to regret everything. But he had seen the impossible and no one and nothing could take that away from him.

"What will you do differently when you get home? I'm never dating another married man."

"I don't know." He didn't want to break up with Doug, but he wanted there to be more than just convenience. He wanted to be valued. "Maybe I need to be more like you and make things happen instead of waiting for them to happen to me."

He could propose to Doug. If he said then no, then that would be it. Saxon would move on. He didn't want to be taken for granted or stay just because it was convenient for both of them to have what was effectively a part-time relationship. He deserved more.

While they'd discussed marriage, that was as far as it had gotten. And it was always a prickly conversation, in part because Doug always brought up Saxon's parents and how much they hated him. It didn't matter that it wasn't just Doug, but every boyfriend because they were male.

If he kept waiting for his parent's approval, he'd never get married.

"So we've both got something to live for," she said.

He grinned, understanding what she'd done. Made him think of home and the reasons to fight and live. Brian had been wrong about Viv; she was smart and determined. That she had money to back it up didn't make her lazy.

He went through every pocket in his bag. Tucked inside a waterproof pouch, he found some matches. He held them up. "Are we going full cave person and carrying fire brands?"

"Why not?"

He could think of a few reasons why not. "Ecologically fragile environment that should be on a world heritage list?"

"We're fighting for our lives."

Were their lives more important than this Cretaceous fragment? In the grand scheme of things, maybe neither mattered. Two humans meant nothing, and dinosaurs had been extinct for millions of years. That there were now a few extant species was an anomaly that no one would miss, because no one even knew it here.

He repacked and then helped Viv down before securing her arm to her chest. She winced but didn't say anything. He gave her the pain pills, and she kept them in her injured hand.

"What do you think would burn well?" He handed her the torch. The pick he kept looped over his wrist.

"It all seems dry."

"No rain." Whatever water there was came from the stream. This far away, the trees were more spread out and there was more grass. He gathered some leaves and sticks, always keeping an eye on the shadows. With the knife, he cut grass and bound it up with the leaves and then finally knotted it all to the stick. It was a pathetic attempt at a fire brand, but it would hopefully be enough.

Viv watched his back while he made three more, not sure if it would be enough or if they'd even burn. Viv put the torch down and picked up a brand, and he lit it for her.

He held his breath until the grass caught and crackled with fire. The sight of the flame was reassuring. Fire kept away predators. This had to work.

"Let's try not to set fire to anything else."

They started toward the cliff near the hole they'd come through. The grasses whipped at his thermal leggings—which were great beneath a snow suit but not great of exploring a primordial forest. They'd been so caught up in the excitement they hadn't really thought it through. While the light in the cavern hadn't changed, it was late, and they were both tired and hurt. The idea of even trying to sleep down here was ridiculous. If he fell asleep, even up a tree, he wouldn't be safe.

He noticed when Viv slowed. For a little while, he matched her pace, but when she slowed again, he hesitated. They couldn't keep stopping and resting.

They couldn't press on forever.

"Come on. We're almost there." But too far away. "We need to keep moving."

"I know. Can I have a mouthful of water? And some more pills?" She opened her hand, and he juggled everything he was holding, putting the unlit firebrands on the ground to open the bottle and get two out. It was too soon, but they both knew that. Was there enough in there they could both take some?

Her body tensed.

He closed his eyes and willed himself to be anywhere but here. When he opened his eyes only a second later, he was still there, and Viv was still watching something behind him. "What's it doing?"

"Watching. Just one and it's in the shadows of the trees. Pills." She opened her mouth, and he put them on her tongue and helped her have a drink. It was only after he slid the water bottle into the side pocket of his backpack that he let himself look. A casual glance as he picked up the firebrands.

The raptor was almost invisible. Motionless as it observed them. Saxon stood and deliberately held its one-eyed gaze.

"Come and get us, fucker." One at a time he could handle.

The raptor edged back as though it hadn't planned on being seen. Saxon stepped forward.

Viv grabbed his backpack. "Let's move on. I don't know how long it's been watching us."

Chittering broke the silence.

Saxon groaned. "And now it's telling all its friends where we are and that we have fire." The raptors were at least as smart as crows. Able to talk, build things…all terrifying when one was on the menu.

"It doesn't know what fire is so it can't tell them anything."

By the end of this never-ending summer day, it would.

For the next hour, Saxon was aware of the one-eyed raptor watching. It didn't bother to hide, but it didn't get close either. He wished it would just attack and get it over with. His pulse was thunder in his ears and he had to remember to relax his jaw.

They'd given up trying to talk unless it was to ask for a sip of water. And the bottle was almost empty.

He wasn't going back to the river to fill it. He'd eat ice if he had to, even though he knew that was something that shouldn't be done because it would lower his core temperature.

"I see the ropes," Viv almost squealed with delight.

Saxon grinned. They were only a hundred meters away. They could do this.

The grass whispered a warning. He turned, and the follower barreled into him, knocking him off balance and onto his back. He exhaled and couldn't take another breath, winded. The raptor leaned over him and pressed a clawed foot over his thigh. The claws sunk into his muscle and he screamed.

CHAPTER 7

The raptor flexed its toes, digging its claws in deeper into Saxon's leg. Saxon swung the unlit brands into its face, smacking it in the side of the head with the damaged eye.

"Get off him." Viv waved the fire at the raptor while keeping her distance.

The raptor flinched but didn't release him.

Saxon drew in a breath and tried not to writhe every time the raptor moved. It was just like playing with a dog, if the dog not so secretly wanted to kill him. For all he knew, it already had, and he was bleeding out. Better it kept its foot where it was instead of making new holes in his thigh.

He held a brand toward her. "Light it and then run for the rope."

"I'm not going without you."

"I'll catch up." He didn't intend on lying here for long.

The brand in his hand caught. The flames flickered in the raptor's eye. It squinted and made a grab for Saxon's arm and the brand but missed. With only one eye, its depth perception was off. He jabbed the brand toward its face, let it feel the heat and learn what fire was. It turned its head away, as though not sure, then made a grab for the flame and failed.

Saxon shoved the brand beneath its chin, to the skin of its soft throat.

The raptor squealed and leaped back.

Saxon ignored the hot pain in his leg and scrambled up, keeping the fire between him and the raptor. The raptor dodged right, and Saxon mirrored it. He needed to run, not dance. He needed to stop the raptor from following.

Another jab and dodge and then he leaned down and swiped up the two unlit brands. He lit one and tossed it at the raptor. The raptor didn't play catch, and the brand fell in the grass. The grass smoked and then caught fire. Tiny licks of flame raced up each leaf and danced to the next one.

The scientist in him cringed at what he was doing to the pristine prehistoric forest. The man who wanted to survive didn't care. He'd regret it later when he was downing vodka and telling tales no one would believe.

He stepped back and his leg buckled before he caught himself. Running was going to be a problem. The raptor watched the fire and looked at him with something akin to hate in its one amber eye. Its confusion and amazement at the fire wouldn't keep it still for long. He turned and hobbled. Blood trickled down his leg and wet his sock. He wasn't going to stop and examine the wound. Looking would only slow him down, not magically heal the damage.

And if he was bleeding out, looking wouldn't change that either.

After several seconds, he realized that if his femoral artery was punctured, he'd be dead already. That didn't change the sickening squish of his sock with each pained step or the need to keep checking over his shoulder. The fire spread, leaping over the grass and spreading toward the trees, pushing the one-eyed raptor back.

Bone-deep loathing swamped him. How could he?

How could he not?

He caught up with Viv because she was standing still, waiting for him. "Come on."

He glanced back—the other raptor now couldn't be seen behind the flames and smoke. Where was it? He glanced around and finally realized why Viv had stopped. They were ten meters from the ropes. But the harnesses were missing, and three raptors were waiting.

"They ate the climbing gear," Viv said, her voice low, pissed off, and afraid. If she'd been holding a gun, Saxon would've back away. She looked like she wanted to rip the raptors apart with her one good hand.

Viv had been right—the raptors had known exactly where they were going, and they'd done their best to destroy their way out. They didn't need harnesses, as they could still climb out by wrapping the rope around in a makeshift harness when they got high enough and had a long enough tail. But how were they going to get past the raptors to get to the ropes?

Something shot out of the forest just in front of them. He held the brand out, but the raptor ignored him and ran to its friends. No doubt to tell them all about fire.

The flames heated Saxon's skin, and the smoke stung his eyes. Tears formed but dried before they could fall. He couldn't muster the anger or hope. There was nothing left but the need to get away. If this place went up, the roof might come down, and he had no idea if the tunnels they'd used to get here would collapse. He hoped it wouldn't burn, not just because he wanted out, but because this place was a miracle, the eighth wonder of the world. He had enough left to recognize the magnificence of the small dinosaurs that had been frozen in time for millennia.

But if they had to die so he could live, then so be it. The age of dinosaurs had ended. These guys hadn't got the memo.

"What now?"

"Same plan. We climb out of here." There was no other option except quit and die and he wasn't ready for that. "All we have to do to climb up, and then we can call the base. Then everything would be fine.

"I can't climb."

"You can. I'll rig something up." He'd get them both out of here. Her parents would be pissed if he returned without her.

"We can't even get to the rope." Her voice became ragged. "They knew."

He nodded, wishing she'd been wrong and that the raptors had been dumb. "Yeah...but we came prepared." He waved the fire brand.

"All we have is fire. And they don't seem too worried that their world is burning."

"We have pain pills."

She frowned at him.

"They like chocolate. Maybe if we scatter the pills, they'll eat them."

"That will take hours to work."

"You don't know that." But she was probably right again.

"And you don't know that they'll eat them, or that they'll have any effect."

"True. But the other option is we sit here and eat them all, and I'm not dying down here." Not when they were so close. "We need to live so we can write the papers and Brian and Carmel didn't die in vain."

"I'm not wasting pills that might not work on the raptors when we might need them. And I don't want to kill them. They're dinosaurs." She spoke the last work with such reverence that he couldn't argue with her.

There were dinosaurs back in the world...it was just unfortunate that they were trying to hunt them and keep them in a pen for later. He smiled at her, though it felt more like a grimace. Here he was doing anything to survive, and she wanted to protect the animals. Maybe she was a better scientist, and a better person, than him. He'd been right about Brian from the moment they'd met. Well-regarded and well-known, and a total dick.

Neither of them moved, but they couldn't stay still forever. Even the raptors knew that. Saxon glanced at the cliff with its ledges and hand holds. They might be able to get up a few meters and make their way across, then he remembered Viv's arm was broken. She wouldn't be able climb over one-handed.

She glanced at the cliff and nodded. "I'd rather have a wall at my back than be encircled by raptors."

While it wasn't a plan, it was all they had. So they angled toward the rock as they edged closer to the waiting raptors. The raptors watched, then fanned out—no doubt they had a plan too. Would they try to herd the humans back to the pen or just go for the kill?

Neither option was calming.

One raptor darted toward the gap between Saxon and the cliff. Saxon lunged with the fire. Viv stayed close to him, almost back to back. The raptors chirped and clicked, their heads tilting as though acknowledging or answering. None got close enough to be burned.

Another standoff.

He and Viv would have to break first. Ten meters—that was all that stood between them and freedom. He could almost taste the frost on his tongue and feel the icy wind on his cheeks.

"The fire you lit is getting closer to us."

Saxon didn't risk glancing over his shoulder. He trusted her. "I shouldn't have done that."

"Probably not. But I'd have done the same."

Her words didn't soothe his conscience. They were running out of options and time. His blood-wet pant leg clung to his thigh, and every step tore something inside of his leg. If he stumbled, the raptors would be on him, and he wouldn't be given the opportunity to get up.

"We're going to inch toward the ropes." He didn't think the raptors would let them get there, but it was better to keep moving; that would force the raptors to keep moving and thinking too.

"Okay. And when we get there?"

He wouldn't have the time to rig anything up unless they were off the ground. He risked a glance at the rock wall. "We need to get on to one of the ledges. Off the ground." Then he'd have a few minutes to think. He could get them both out of here.

He crept his foot forward, trying to be as sneaky as he could. The raptor in front of him wasn't stupid. It lunged as though to stop him. Saxon jabbed the brand. He still had the torch and pick, but he preferred having half a meter of burning stick between him and the snappy jaws. When the raptor darted to the side, he took another step forward. Viv was close enough to his back that he could feel every move she made.

She swung as another raptor attacked. "They're getting braver."

"Or desperate." Why though? There were other food sources. Why fight so hard for something that they hadn't even known existed until earlier today?

"Yeah...do you think they're running out of food?"

"I don't know. I haven't had time to think about it." Another ten centimeters closer.

"I did. While I was pretending to be dead. I think it's getting too warm in here."

"To warm?" It wasn't that warm. Maybe twenty-five Celsius?

"Think about it. If the ice sheets are melting, then this place might be warming too. That would explain why so many trees looked unhealthy. And why there are so few animals."

"Maybe we just didn't see them."

"Come on. I know you've done plenty of field work."

"So you're planning a return trip?" He swung the brand, trying to push the raptor back so he could gain another few centimeters.

"Of course. We need to save, and study, this place. Next time though, I'll come as though it's a safari."

"With raptors instead of lions."

"Exactly. My family will be thrilled to fund this research."

Of course they would, and Viv would lead the project. Saxon didn't even care as long as he was involved. "You'll invite me back?"

"Yes."

The four raptors rushed them, getting in close and kicking, hoping for a strike. Viv grunted and knocked into him. He shoved the brand into an open mouth and then kept pushing even as the raptor backed away. Then he let go. The raptor tossed its head, struggling to get the brand out of it mouth, groping with it claws as it choked and burned and, after what felt like hours but was only seconds, fell over. It's dying scrabble continued as it writhed on the ground, the air filling with the scent of barbeque.

Saxon switched the heavy plastic torch to his other hand and gripped the pick as he started forward. Viv wasn't behind him. He glanced behind. "Come on."

"Yeah."

She'd dropped her brand and the grass at her feet was on fire. His heart dropped.

"Viv?"

She turned. Both hands were red and pressed over her lower abdomen. "I dropped the pills."

"It's fine. We can get you out of here."

She shook her head. "No, you can't. I'll go into shock in a few minutes."

"I'll bandage—"

"Behind you!"

Saxon turned and shone the torch in the raptor's eyes, but it ran and crashed into him. They didn't fear the torch anymore. He stumbled into the cliff, scraping skin off his elbow. He swore. "We can do this."

He wasn't quitting until they were actually eating him.

"I'm holding my guts in." She kicked as a raptor got close. "Just grab the pills for me."

"No."

"Please." She looked at him with wide, glassy eyes.

Saxon eyed the bottle, then dodged around her to scoop it up. A raptor snapped at where his hand had been only seconds before. But he didn't unscrew the cap and hand it to her the way she wanted. He used his other hand to swing the torch at another headbutt attempt.

She held out her hand, her fingers slick with blood. "Give the bottle to me."

A tail struck his knee, then another. He couldn't whack the tails with the torch or pick; they were too quick. And every strike knocked him off balance. Viv stumbled, and he caught her, dragging her close to the wall.

A raptor kicked at him and he narrowly dodged only to have another crash into his thigh. They weren't trying to kill him, but they were trying to bring him down. Keeping Viv close, he edged toward a small lip only half a meter above the ground. If they could get up there, it would be a start. He put the torch on the ledge but let the pick swing from his wrist.

"Come on. One big step." He made sure she was leaning against the cliff before he took the step up first. The ledge wasn't even twenty centimeters wide. He shuffled into a reasonable position, holding the cliff with one hand, and then grabbing Viv under her broken arm. He wasn't leaving her down there, even if she was dying.

She cried out, but assisted, scrambling up. "Stop trying to help me."

The raptors stared up at them. Too much intelligence flickered in their eyes.

The backpack was too bulky, throwing off his balance and not letting him press hard enough against the cliff. He didn't have the hands to hold it, but all the samples, the photos, the evidence were in there.

She tipped her head against the rock and stared at the raptors as they stared back. "What now, genius?"

They had about eight meters of moving sideways to get to the ropes. Saxon shrugged out of the backpack. He took a last sip of water and then handed the bottle to Viv. "How are you feeling?"

"Cold, nauseated. If there was an ambulance waiting at the top, I might have a chance. But we've got to walk out of the caves and then call for help. It'll take them at least an hour to get to us. It's not the cut. It's the blood loss."

Saxon tried not to think about his leg. The flow of blood seemed to have slowed, but he was sure that as soon as he started climbing whatever had clotted and scabbed would rip open. He glanced at Viv's stomach and her blood-drenched clothing. "I'm not leaving you down here."

He couldn't bear the losing another colleague, a friend, to the raptors. But he didn't know how he'd get her out either when he knew she was right about her injuries. Maybe about his too. He had no idea how much blood he'd lost, or would continue to lose, while he waited for help. He stared at the burning grass, the way it had jumped to the trees.

They'd ruined this place.

"Dragging my corpse will only slow you down. And you're hurt bad." She dropped her gaze to his ripped and stained pants. "One of us needs to get out. If it's not me, then it has to be you."

"We can try."

"No, we can't. I'm barely standing. Just give me the damn pills."

The raptors lifted the heads and sniffed at their feet. Saxon kicked at them. They needed to get higher because if Viv lay down here, they'd drag her off and eat her. While he knew that was why she wanted the pills, he didn't want that end for her. What would happen when he returned to the surface alone?

They should have all been getting out of here after having a quick look around. None of them had expected dinosaurs. Denying the raptors one more meal was all they had. "If we go up a little, they won't be able to reach you."

She stared at him, then the raptors, and nodded. They didn't need to say more. Saxon glanced to his left and right and up, trying to determine what would be the easiest course to get Viv somewhere safe, while not falling into the waiting maws.

The raptors bobbed and danced, chirping.

The most suitable ledge was in the wrong direction. "I need to swap places with you."

"How do we do that?"

"I'm going to step around you." He handed her the pill bottle. "Don't take them yet."

She nodded.

"Press up against the wall." He found a hand hold and carefully went around her.

Pain shot through his calf. His fingers tightened on the rock. The raptor tugged, its whole weight hanging off his leg. His grip slipped. It was going drag him down, and once he was down, he'd never get up again.

CHAPTER 8

Saxon gritted his teeth and tried to shake the raptor off, skin and muscle tearing. Viv kicked the torch at it. There was a thunk as plastic connected with raptor head, and it let go. He didn't stop and check his injury, just reached up to the next hand hold and the next ledge.

He sat there, one and a half meters off the ground, and felt a whole lot better about life. Now all he had to do was get Viv up here.

"Are you okay?"

"Yeah, it mostly had my pants." That was a lie, but she had more than enough to worry about. They were never getting the torch back. One weapon down.

"How am I supposed to get up there?"

"I'm going to help you. It's nice up here." Wide enough to sit and watch the raptors and take a moment.

"What about the bag?"

"If you can't toss it to me, it stays."

She glanced at the bag, shoved the pill bottle deep into the sling, then hooked the bag with her toe until it was in a position that she could grab it. "Incoming."

Her throw went wide and catching it nearly sent him over the edge, but he recovered and set it down next to him. The next bit was going to be harder, and from the grim set to her face, she knew it too.

The raptors seemed to understand what he had planned and started worrying at Viv's feet and legs.

"You need to step out high like I did. There's enough grip on that knob."

"How do I hold on?"

Saxon got on his belly and stretched out. "Grab my hand."

Viv lifted her leg, and the raptor snapped at the air. "I don't want to spill out." Her voice wobbled.

"Keep your broken arm hand pressed hard to your stomach and stretch." How bad was the wound that she was worried about her insides falling out? He extended his arm, his own hand bloody, dirty, scratched, and scraped.

She wedged her foot onto the rock. "If you drop me…"

"I won't." If she went, they both went. He made the silent vow.

Pressed close to the wall, she reached out her hand. He wriggled as far over as he dared and clasped her hand. "Get your other leg up. Find a foot hold. Now!"

She got her other foot up. It took all of Saxon's strength to counteract her wobble. But she was above raptor height, just. "Keep coming, a little closer to me."

"You did it in two steps."

"I had two hands." And ten years' experience. He needed her to hurry before his grip weakened. But he couldn't say that. If she panicked, she'd be careless.

Carefully, she picked another foot hold and then another. The raptors' chittering increased. He couldn't look at them though—he had to watch her and concentrate on the way her weight moved.

He needed to get off his belly.

"I'm going to get slowly to my knees, and you're going to come the rest of the way over." She gave a tiny nod, her cheek almost pressed to the rock. Her breathing was fast and shallow, and he worried that it would be her grip that gave out first. He moved as smoothly as he could. "Okay, last bit."

She made it over and slumped against the wall, clutching at her gut.

Now that they were safe, he could check out the wounds. Maybe it wasn't that bad. A bit of blood loss, but nothing more. "Want me to look?"

Viv gave him a dead-eyed stare. "Sure." She separated her fingers. He expected to see blood and muscle, but all he saw were slippery intestines. "I can feel it, Saxon. You don't have to lie. No more lies. I shouldn't have hidden my relationship with Brian."

He stared at her wound, not sure how she'd got this far with it. And he had no idea how he could help her. She needed more than what he had in his bag, than what they had in the rest of their gear.

"I get it." He might have done the same if he'd been involved with an older, influential expert.

"Can you take my necklace off? Give it my mum."

Saxon swallowed. "What do I tell her?"

"The truth. That I discovered dinosaurs. Make sure they name them after me."

"I'll do my best." He nodded. He had no doubt that the Anstruthers would get a dino named after them.

She slid down to sitting and made sure her legs were tucked up. "How bad in your leg."

He laughed, like his leg mattered when she was dying. "Which one?"

"Both."

"I haven't looked at either." He feared what he'd find.

"Maybe you should, before you go up."

But if he looked, and it was horrific, he may not even try. Even as he thought it, his calf stung and throbbed and sent a half a dozen other unpleasant sensations to his brain. He didn't need more information. "I'm sure it will be fine."

"I'll look and do what I can. You need to make it out."

Saxon pulled the bag over and took out the first-aid kit. While he did that, Viv took another two tablets.

"I'm sorry." He didn't know what else to say. This whole thing was his fault, and it was a crushing weight.

"You didn't kick me. Fuck. I thought I was going to make it. I thought I was going to get out of here and have a tale to tell." Her voice broke. "Can you find paper and take a note?"

He got paper and a pencil while she wrapped his calf as best she could with one hand. He took down her message to her family. When she was done, she took the paper and signed it before handing it back. Bloody fingerprints marked the paper, his and hers. He folded the note and put it into the zip pocket of his pants, along with the necklace, so they wouldn't get lost.

His calf didn't feel any better. The raptors were still below, and the air was hazy from the grass fire that was burning itself out. The smoke made his eyes gritty and hot.

Viv crunched another two tablets like they were trail mix.

"Are they helping?"

"No. But they aren't not helping. Will you sit with me a bit?" She leaned her head on his shoulder.

"Yeah."

He watched the smoke coil up to the ice roof and listened to the raptors' chitter. Then closed his eyes for a moment. When he startled awake, he was the only human alive.

"Viv?"

He gently shook her, and her arm flopped aside, revealing the true extent of her injury. His stomach rolled, but his mouth was closed and there was nothing to come up. He was lucky to have woken.

A chirp made him look over at the first ledge he'd been on. A raptor stood there staring at him, then it jumped. It didn't make it across, but it came close enough that his heart lurched.

With help, another one climbed onto the ledge and attempted the jump. They were helping each other, figuring out the best way to get to him…and Viv. He lay her down, not sure if she was high enough, but knowing there was nothing more he could do for her. Intestines slid from the open wound. He coughed, gagging, and looked away.

Every part of his body hurt. He started to repack the bag, then stopped. He didn't need most of this stuff, or the extra weight. He took a few of the samples and the camera and shoved them into another pocket. The container with the dead centipede in he left with Viv, along with the remains of the first-aid kit. There was a better medical kit waiting for him, along with more food and water. All he had to do was make it up.

The raptor grabbed the rock ledge he was on. Its claws slid over the rock and it fell.

Saxon wouldn't be able to go down and across. He would to have to go up, risking a greater fall. Viv's words rung in his head. One of them needed to make it back, to tell the world. Warn the world.

It had to be him.

He clasped Viv's still warm hand—there was no pulse, no breath. She'd need an ambulance within minutes. Anger simmered in his blood; they'd been so close. Now he was going to have to tell her family.

He tried to imagine how his parents would feel if they were told he'd died in the Antarctic. But he couldn't imagine them being sad—they'd make some comment about he was always running off and doing something stupid. For all that they hated Doug, he'd probably agree with them. He hadn't wanted Saxon to go at all.

Saxon gritted his teeth. He would survive and study the dinosaurs and they could all go to hell. He used the anger as fuel.

He found a suitable toe hold and started making his way over to the ropes. He went up only if he needed, focusing only on getting across. He didn't look down, to where the raptors followed beneath him. It wasn't until he had a hand on the rope and he was standing on a ledge that he let himself take one final look at the cave.

A few hours and four humans had killed and burned and changed this place forever.

The ice cave had done the same to him.

Sweat made the open wounds on his legs sting and he was sure they'd ripped open and were bleeding again. But he wasn't stopping, not for anything. He was sure if he fell asleep again, he wouldn't wake up, and if by some chance he did, he'd be too weak to make the climb.

There were two ropes and not a carabiner in sight or harness in sight. He glanced up at the hole in the ice. It was only a few hundred meters...but he knew it would feel like more while he was climbing. He wasn't very good at free climbing; that was Doug's thing. Saxon preferred having a rope.

A raptor tugged on the end of rope in his hand as though to dislodge him. They just wouldn't give up. He glanced back at where Viv lay. At least they were leaving her alone…not that she'd feel a thing now.

For several minutes, he debated the best way to climb. He could make a harness out of one of the ropes, but he had no other equipment and it would be a false sense of security. This was the kind of rock face that made for a good free climb. There were plenty of hand holds. The only problem would be at the top. The hole wasn't near the wall. He'd be dangling like a fish on a hook for the last ten meters.

He assessed the climb again and went through options, knowing he was stalling, because once he started, he wouldn't be able to stop. He'd weaken and tire and give up if he wasn't careful. He'd walk up the wall as far as he could, then he'd have to climb like he was in gym class. Hand over hand, using his knees—that would be the worst part.

He glanced down at the raptors clicking only three meters below. He saw the rubble and the flattened grass where the four of them had tramped into the forest full of hope and wonder and excitement. He didn't let himself look up to the hole, to safety.

He'd stare at the wall and walk his way up. One step at a time. He grabbed the rope, took a breath, and made the first step, then the second. It wasn't long before every part of him screamed and sweated. He kept going, pausing to catch his breath when he reached ledges, but never letting go of the rope in case it swung away—or was dragged away.

The rope jerked as a raptor toyed with the end. His foot slipped. If he fell now, he was dead, and for half a heartbeat, it was almost tempting. No more pain. No more anything—that was the scary thought.

He wanted so much more than nothing.

He forced himself to keep moving to the next ledge and then the one after, always only looking a meter a head, small goals. His hands stung, and his shoulders burned.

Gradually, the air chilled. A breeze dusted his face.

He allowed himself to rest for a few breaths on what looked like the last narrow ledge before he had to climb the rope. This time, he didn't look down, only up. The hole was so close. But his hands were shredded and there was nothing he could do about it until he got through the hole. While he caught his breath, he tipped his face to the breeze and breathed it in, clearing the smoke tainted air from his lungs and wishing he could erase the day in much the same way.

Finally, he reached that point where if he didn't get moving, he'd sit down, and he couldn't do that. He prepared for the rope climb, giving his arms a shake, knowing that he needed them even if he was taking most of his weight on his legs. He pulled up, then clamped the rope between his feet, stood, and reached up again. He made his way up like a caterpillar, crunch and stretch, crunch and stretch, concentrating on the next few feet of rope.

The breeze grew colder.

Then when he reached up, his hands were just below the ice. With shaking legs, he paused. He had to get over the lip somehow. He pushed up, sticking his head through the hole. He'd only get one chance to do this. Sweat rolled down his back as he reached over the lip to grasp the other rope—his own was pulled tight with no room to get his fingers under—and he gave it a tug to be sure it would hold then grabbed it with his other hand too. He brought his legs up, clamped the rope between his feet and pushed up, then he was halfway through the hole.

A tiny part of him had been hoping for rescue. For someone to realize everything had gone horribly wrong. But there was no one there, just the abandoned equipment. He pulled himself the rest of the way through the hole. He sucked in the cold air, relief washing through his shaking limbs and making him gasp. Then he slid a few inches back toward the hole. The warm air from the below cavern had turned the ice to glass. There was no grip. In a rush of panic, he hauled himself over to the wall on his belly. He tried to stand but he couldn't, his calf cramped and burned and bled. His other thigh was in no better shape. He'd left a trail of blood.

Gripping the rope tight, he closed his eyes. He still had to make it to where they'd left the bulk of their things. Where they'd planned to stop for the night. He shivered as the cold air bit through his thin clothes. It wasn't freezing in here, but it wasn't that warm either.

He had to keep moving and get to the food and the water and his suit before the cold sucked everything from him.

Saxon got to his knees and crawled up the tunnel, leaving a blood smear every time he put his hand down. He almost sobbed when he saw his gear. His suit. He'd get warm and then keep moving.

Movement in his suit caught his eye. He watched the suit bump and wriggle for a moment before a centipede lifted its head. Saxon blinked, remembering his first discovery in the ice tunnels, then slowly looked behind him. His trail of blood had drawn them out. He was their next meal.

CHAPTER 9

Whether it was the warmth of his body, or the scent of blood and the raw meat of his open wounds, Saxon didn't know. But there were centipedes scuttling up the tunnel, stopping to taste his blood on the ice and dropping off the ceiling to join in.

If he stopped to shake out his suit, they'd be on him. And while one had barely been tolerable, there were a dozen, maybe more. He couldn't stop. With a sob and wrench of will, he forced himself on. They weren't in the outer tunnels where it was cold.

He shouldn't be in the outer tunnels where it was cold without a suit. The dangers had been drilled into them. Hypothermia and frost bite could all set in fast at sub-zero temperatures. He wanted to grab the backpack near the suit but didn't trust that it was centipede free. All he could do was keep going to where they'd left the rest of their equipment.

The ice bit into his hands, every movement making his thigh cramp and twist and burn as though it were tearing apart.

He kept checking over his shoulder, but they were still following his bloody trail.

Stopping would be bad.

The centipedes would get him, and he'd get cold—which would kill him first? Already the sweat of the climb was chilling on his skin. His body would be cooling even though he hadn't realized yet. The centipedes were obvious, but the cold was silent and sneaky. He'd been so worried about raptors and escaping he hadn't thought about what was waiting.

His hands hurt too much, his palms raw from rope and ice, so he dropped to his forearms. Past the place where he'd first seen the centipedes and been so excited. On toward to the fork where Brian and he had argued. That fatal desire to go deeper. He blinked, refusing to allow himself the luxury of tears or sorrow. There'd be time for that later.

Again he checked, hoping the centipedes were put off by the cold, but they followed, not wanting to lose their feast. Saxon dragged himself on, shivering now, knowing he was in danger if got colder. In their gear there'd be sleeping bags, foil blankets, and chemical heat packs. Food and water.

He sat next to the bag. It had been easy to put it on and hike this morning—or was it yesterday?—but now he had no chance. He couldn't even walk.

But he couldn't leave the bag. Without it he was dead, and he hadn't worked this hard to die so close to safety. He had to be the one to survive. He'd promised Viv.

Frustration exploded within him and he yelled at the centipedes. At everything. No words, just an anguished cry that left his throat as raw as the rest of him.

He drew in a sharp, cold breath. "Fuck off."

They didn't, of course. They scuttled closer, waiting for the moment where they could swamp him en mass. He was tempted to throw something at them, but Brian had done something to make them attack, so Saxon didn't.

All he could do was keep going toward the colder parts of the tunnels and hope that it wasn't cold enough to finish him. He was running on the fumes of hope and little else. He hooked one arm through the strap of his backpack and dragged himself and the bag onward. He lied to himself, that it was just a little farther. He was only a little cold, not deadly cold.

He'd stop soon, go through the bag, and have something to eat and drink and more importantly, contact the base. He just had to get away from the centipedes.

He repeated that to himself with every meter he dragged himself, always checking behind. Never surprised that they were still there in his bloody tracks. The ice shredded the knees of his pants and new grazes formed, spilling fresh blood, but he didn't stop. When his teeth started rattling so hard, he could barely think, that was when he stopped.

He couldn't get any colder, centipedes or not.

His hands were cold and cramped and clumsy as he freed the sleeping bag from its straps. It took too long, but there were three centipedes behind him. Only three, and they weren't moving. He'd finally reached a place where it was too cold for them...until he lit the stove and ate.

Gritting his teeth against the pain, he got into the sleeping bag. He'd wanted the relief to be instant, but it wasn't. And he wasn't safe yet. Like a caterpillar, he kept going; the closer he got to the entrance, the better. It would be easier for base to find him.

But really, he just wanted as much distance as he could put between him and everything else.

The wind in the tunnel nipped at his cheeks. It hadn't been that windy when they'd entered. It had been a beautiful, sunny and sparkling white. He ignored the tightening of his gut and wriggled around the bend.

A few more meters and then he'd stop.

His mouth was dry, and he was still shaking. From the cold or from hunger?

He needed to rest, but if he stopped, would he ever get going?

This negotiation with himself continued for another couple of meters. Then he decided that a drink and a bite of an energy bar were what he needed. If he stopped being able to think clearly, that was just as dangerous as anything else.

He found a bottle of water and drank more than a sip and ate a whole protein bar while nestled deep in the sleeping back. Warming up meant his hands started stinging, along with his knees. Every ache sharpened. He tipped his head back against

the icy wall and checked down the tunnel for centipedes—
nothing.

He was alone.

He sighed and closed his eyes.

Snapping them open just as fast. He needed to reach the entrance and set off the emergency beacon. The idea of moving, of hurting himself more, was almost too much. So he bandaged his hands as best he could, then pulled on a spare set of gloves and balaclava. Stalling so he didn't have to move, but calling it practical, survival.

Then he started off again, dragging the bag, crawling up and out of the mountain.

The wind became stronger as he drew closer to the entrance.

He squinted, not sure why he couldn't see the sky…his stomach sunk.

White out.

A storm had swept in. He lay down, unable to go on when there was no point. He lay there, curled up like a dying bug, his body broken and bleeding, knowing he'd have to wait until the storm blew itself out. That could be in an hour or it could be several days.

He didn't know what to do.

So he lay there listening to the howling, trying not to go to sleep even though it was whispering seductively in his ear.

Finally, he made a decision. He moved out of the wind and set off the beacon. Then he ate several more snacks, because there was no point in saving them and since he was going to have to wait out the storm, he might as well not do it hungry.

With a full belly, he slid deep into the sleeping bag and closed his eyes.

They may not reach him in time, but they'd know something was wrong. Maybe he'd get lucky...

CHAPTER 10

Saxon remembered being jostled, glimpses of blue skies, and the heavy thump of a helicopter in his lungs. The rest was all dreams...or nightmares. He ran from tiny raptors and monstrous centipedes. He couldn't find anyone; he was lost and alone.

He drew in a breath and this time something was different. He was able to drag himself out of the dreams that wanted to pull him back under with their claws. He blinked and saw only white. But he wasn't cold. He blinked again, and the white resolved into a ceiling. However, he still didn't know where he was. He stared at the ceiling for a bit and listened to the rhythmic beep of a machine. Then figured he must be in a hospital. He must have gotten hypothermia...but that knowledge didn't sit right.

But something was wrong with him.

The machine kept beeping.

Every time he blinked, he saw the raptors watching him from the shadows. Why was he in the hospital? Fear pumped his heart harder, and he tried to sit up. His hands were unusable, so bundled up in bandages. There was a drip in his arm.

Centipedes.

Raptors.

Death.

His breathing was too loud and rasping. Where was he? Was he still in Antarctica? He had to be. He pulled back the blanket, using both hands like salad tongs and stopped. He was in a hospital gown, but that wasn't the worst. His thigh was completely bandaged.

No. No. No.

He moved his other leg. It should've been a dream, but sure enough, his calf was hidden with bandages.

His breathing came in hard pants as if once again he was being chased through the prehistoric forest beneath the ice. It wasn't a nightmare.

The door swung open and a man in a suit walked in. He pulled over the hospital tray, so it was across the bed and in front of Saxon, as though to trap him. Saxon wanted to tell him to leave, but he needed answers and this man looked like he had them, though he wouldn't hand them out for free.

The man sat on the edge of the bed like they were old friends. Saxon was ninety-nine percent sure they'd never met before this.

"Saxon Smith…" the man didn't seem to want an answer. "You had quite the expedition."

He nodded. "Who are you again? I seem to have forgotten." Maybe he'd forgotten a whole lot of things. But he seemed to know his own birthday and name, even if he wasn't sure of the date or where he was.

"I work for the government."

"CSIRO?"

"No. And it's not important." He pulled several small clear bags out of his briefcase and laid them on the tray. In the bags were Viv's letter and an assortment of photos. Then one small cannister, the kind hospitals used for piss samples, except this one contained a tooth. He gave it a rattle. "The doctors found this embedded in your calf."

The tooth rattled as it was set down. It wasn't brown like the fossils in museums, but white. Saxon stared at the raptor tooth, smooth on one side, serrated on the other. It had snapped off at the root. He'd seen fossils just like it…raptors lost their teeth in prey and grew new ones, much like sharks.

"I think you need to start at the beginning and leave nothing out."

Saxon stared at the photos; they didn't seem real.

"Three people are dead. You are a likely suspect."

Saxon snapped his gaze up. "I didn't kill anyone."

The man tapped the photo of the dinosaurs. "Come on. If this goes public, who's going to believe it?"

His mouth dried. "What do you want? Do you work for the Anstruthers?"

The man laughed. "No. I work for people much bigger than them."

"You said the government."

"There's more than one." He smiled. "You must be smart. Got your degree, got on the trip. Survived. So I'm assuming you'll grasp this pretty quick. You can be at the cutting edge of science if you cooperate."

"Or?" There was a price. A threat that was being whispered. The kind he should understand.

"There are a few options, but you'd get to choose, of course. You could die of a mystery bacterium, face twenty to life for the murder of three people, or find yourself medicated and raving about dinosaurs."

They weren't really choices.

They were preparing to stitch him up for murder to make the dinosaurs go away. If he talked, he'd disappear and be so drugged up he wouldn't know his own name. No one would believe there was dinosaurs running around beneath the Antarctic ice.

"Where am I?"

"Safe."

"If your boss is so important, why do you need me?"

That smile again. "They don't. But they prefer to invite people in and give them what they want—it's tidier."

Saxon nodded as if he understood perfectly. His head was still too foggy. The lights hummed and somewhere outside his room people laughed. The machine kept beeping.

"Does anyone know where I am?"

The man didn't answer that. He didn't need to.

"Is this the kind of research I can never talk about?"

"For a while. We don't want public panic or certain people bringing in private teams and making a mess."

Viv's family. They had the money to fund trips and something like the cavern couldn't be fenced off; it would be open to the scientific community.

Saxon leaned back against the pillows and took a moment to collect his thoughts. The raptors chased each one down and tore it to shreds. What was the point in surviving only to disappear or worse?

The government man was waiting as though he knew Saxon needed time but couldn't be left alone. This wasn't the first time the man had done this. What other marvels had been hidden?

The itch to know burned beneath his skin. He'd never publish papers and never be well known. He'd never end up like Brian. His family would forever sneer at the work he couldn't talk about. Doug would wonder why he kept going away—though no doubt this man would have a cover story for him to tell. He stared at the tooth. It didn't matter what they wanted. It didn't even really matter what this man wanted.

It was his life and he was alive to live it.

Saxon leaned forward and picked up the container. He'd become a dinosaur expert and do the work he loved. "This is a raptor tooth. We found a cave beneath the ice. A remnant forest." A nightmare…a wonder. And it was his to explore. "A Cretaceous fragment."

The End

 SEVERED**PRESS**

CHECK OUT OTHER GREAT DINOSAUR BOOKS

FLIPSIDE
by JAKE BIBLE

The year is 2046 and dinosaurs are real.

Time bubbles across the world, many as large as one hundred square miles, turn like clockwork, revealing prehistoric landscapes from the Cretaceous Period.

They reveal the Flipside.

Now, thirty years after the first Turn, the clockwork is breaking down as one of the world's powers has decided to exploit the phenomenon for their own gain, possibly destroying everything then and now in the process.

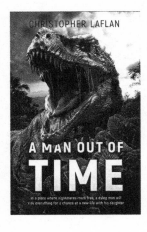

A MAN OUT OF TIME
by Christopher Laflan

Five years after the Chinese Axis detonated an unknown weapon of mass destruction off the southern coast of the United States, Special Ops Sergeant John Crider and the members of Shadow Company have finally captured what they all hope will lead to the end of the war. Unfortunately, the population within the United States is no longer sustainable. In an effort to stabilize the economy, the government enacts the Cryonics Act. One hundred years in suspended animation, all debt forgiven, and a chance at a less crowded future are too good to pass up for John and his young daughter.

Except not everything always goes as planned as Sergeant John Crider finds himself pitted against a land of prehistoric monsters genetically resurrected from the fossil record, murderous inhabitants, and a future he never wanted.

CHECK OUT OTHER GREAT DINOSAUR BOOKS

PRIMORDIA
by **Greig Beck**

Ben Cartwright, former soldier, home to mourn the loss of his father stumbles upon cryptic letters from the past between the author, Arthur Conan Doyle and his great, great grandfather who vanished while exploring the Amazon jungle in 1908.

Amazingly, these letters lead Ben to believe that his ancestor's expedition was the basis for Doyle's fantastical tale of a lost world inhabited by long extinct creatures. As Ben digs some more he finds clues to the whereabouts of a lost notebook that might contain a map to a place that is home to creatures that would rewrite everything known about history, biology and evolution.

But other parties now know about the notebook, and will do anything to obtain it. For Ben and his friends, it becomes a race against time and against ruthless rivals.

In the remotest corners of Venezuela, along winding river trails known only to lost tribes, and through near impenetrable jungle, Ben and his novice team find a forbidden place more terrifying and dangerous than anything they could ever have imagined.

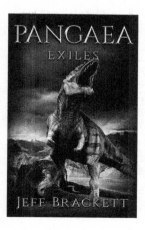

PANGAEA EXILES
by **Jeff Brackett**

Tried and convicted for his crimes, Sean Barrow is sent into temporal exile—banished to a time so far before recorded history that there is no chance that he, or any other criminal sent back, has any chance of altering history.

Now Sean must find a way to survive more than 200 million years in the past, in a world populated by monstrous creatures that would rend him limb from limb if they got the chance. And that's just his fellow prisoners.

The dinosaurs are almost as bad.

CHECK OUT OTHER GREAT DINOSAUR BOOKS

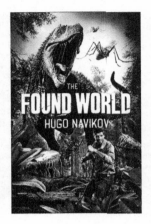

THE FOUND WORLD
by **Hugo Navikov**

A powerful global cabal wants adventurer Brett Russell to retrieve a superweapon stolen by the scientist who built it. To entice him to travel underneath one of the most dangerous volcanoes on Earth to find the scientist, this shadowy organization will pay him the only thing he cares about: information that will allow him to avenge his family's murder.

But before he can get paid, he and his team must enter an underground hellscape of killer plants, giant insects, terrifying dinosaurs, and an army of other predators never previously seen by man.

At the end of this journey awaits a revelation that could alter the fate of mankind ... if they can make it back from this horrifying found world.

HOUSE OF THE GODS
by **Davide Mana**

High above the steamy jungle of the Amazon basin, rise the flat plateaus known as the Tepui, the House of the Gods. Lost worlds of unknown beauty, a naturalistic wonder, each an ecology onto itself, shunned by the local tribes for centuries. The House of the Gods was not made for men.

But now, the crew and passengers of a small charter plane are about to find what was hidden for sixty million years.

Lost on an island in the clouds 10.000 feet above the jungle, surrounded by dinosaurs, hunted by mysterious mercenaries, the survivors of Sligo Air flight 001 will quickly learn the only rule of life on Earth: Extinction.

Made in the USA
Monee, IL
28 July 2021